A Perfect Hoax

A Perfect Hoax

Italo Svevo

Translated by J.G. Nichols

ET REMOTISSIMA PROPE

100 PAGES

100 PAGES

Published by Hesperus Press Limited

4 Rickett Street, London sw6 1ru

www.hesperuspress.com

First published in Italian as *Una burla riuscita* in 1929

This translation first published by Hesperus Press Limited, 2003

Introduction and English language translation of *A Perfect Hoax* © J.G. Nichols, 2003

'Italo Svevo at the British Admiralty' English language translation

© Estelle Gilson, 1993, and reproduced by permission of Carcanet Press Limited

Foreword © Tim Parks, 2003

Designed and typeset by Fraser Muggeridge

Printed in the United Arab Emirates by Oriental Press

ISBN: 1-84391-058-6

CONTENTS

'No one,' wrote the Romanian philosopher Emil Cioran, 'can do without a semblance of immortality, and even less will they deny themselves the right to seek it out in the form of this or that reputation, starting with the literary. Ever since we began to look on death as the absolute end, *everybody writes*.'

Cioran relates a sudden explosion of the desire for literary fame to the decline of religious belief. Mario Samigli, the hero, if we can call him that, of *A Perfect Hoax*, is the kind of person who no doubt prompted the philosopher's reflection. Almost sixty years old, Samigli published a novel forty years earlier to the total indifference of press and public. Yet he continues, in a quiet, dreamy way, to believe himself destined for literary glory. Dividing his dull life between a humdrum office job and a demanding invalid brother, he nevertheless enjoys a perpetual sense of self-satisfaction, because of his illusion. It helps him to live and avoid unpleasant thoughts of death and oblivion. The 'hoax' of the novella's title is a cruel practical joke that will destroy the dreamer's equilibrium and force him to look at reality.

Of course the downside to seeking glory through any public endeavour is the possibility of receiving a bad press. 'Who could ever feel at ease,' the great Swiss writer Robert Walser asked, 'when he attaches importance to the world's proclamations of admiration and distinction?' Samigli spares himself these anxieties by not actually writing or publishing. Instead, he jots down a fable or two every day, as a kind of ⟨illegible⟩ in any work by Svevo, we realise that his real subject is not so much the drama in hand, but the comic perversity of the human mind and its self-deceptive machinations. Of Samigli's self-satisfaction, we are told, 'That era could only remain a happy one so long as he was making an effort to escape from it [that is to become a successful writer]… Fortunately he never found a route that would have taken him away from his great happiness.'

It is 1915 and Italy declares war on Austria. Being one of the only Italians of literary pretensions in Austrian-governed Trieste, Samigli is suddenly terrified and excited by the prospect that he will be persecuted by the Austrian military. Their top generals will read his book of forty years before and condemn or spare him on that basis. In short, he returns to the condition, as anxious as it is ridiculous, of the author awaiting reviews, a figure now seen to be not unlike some Kafkaesque hero desperate for Court or Castle to make up its mind about him. In her biography of her husband, Svevo's wife would write of his state of mind on the publication of his second novel: 'He published it with the anxiety of someone awaiting a final verdict, but once again it was met with icy incomprehension.'

Svevo's novel had been called *Senilità* [*As a Man Grows Older*]. Samigli's book is *Una giovinezza* ['One Man's Youth']. Needless to say, the war ends without the Austrian authorities paying it any attention. 'Disappointed and reassured,' Samigli is just returning to his old, happy life in which the only use for his novel is that of reading it out loud every night to send his sick brother to sleep, when, on the last day of the war, a work colleague, who resents Samigli's literary pretensions, tells him that a German publisher is planning to offer a large sum of money for the publication of *Una giovinezza*. All at once dream and reality coincide, or appear to.

The idea of a tardy and unexpected literary success was very much on Svevo's mind in 1925, when he began work on

A Perfect Hoax. Born in 1860, Italo Svevo's real name was Ettore Schmitz. He grew up speaking Triestine dialect, and only later learnt German and standard Italian. Starting to write in late adolescence, he always used a pseudonym, as if fearing from the outset that there was something unreal about his aspirations.

In the 1890s, two novels published at the author's own expense were met with almost total silence. 'Renunciation was the only course,' he decided, and for twenty years he worked in his father-in-law's industrial paints business and published nothing. Only in 1922, and with great rapidity, did he write his masterpiece, *La coscienza di Zeno* [*The Confessions of Zeno*]. Published in 1923, again at his own expense, it was again largely ignored, until Svevo sent a copy to the man who had once been his private English teacher, James Joyce. In Paris, Joyce aroused the interest of French publishers. Soon afterwards the Italian critics began to wake up. By 1925 the sixty-five year old Svevo was looking at the possibility, but not yet the certainty, of a considerable literary success.

The Austrian generals may have ignored Samigli's old novel, but thanks to his paranoid anxieties, the quality of his fables was much improved ('a literary development he owed to the police'). His endless four- or five-line stories about a man and the flock of sparrows he feeds become a way of mediating between his private world and external reality, a way of recognising his own unwarranted vanity while at the same time keeping it alive precisely by perfecting his ability to describe it in this oblique and ambiguous medium. Here is an example

'A generous man, regularly and for many years, had given breadcrumbs every day to some little birds, convinced that in

*their hearts they loved him for it. The fellow was blind,
otherwise he would have realised that the birds thought him
an idiot from whom, for years, they had been able to steal the
bread without his managing to catch even one of them.'*

As soon as storytelling is seen as a strategy for maintaining the teller's mental equilibrium, it becomes hard not to think of the whole of *A Perfect Hoax* as an attempt on Svevo's part to deal with the upheaval and anxiety of an unexpected literary success that had almost, but not quite, become reality. To keep his feet firmly on the ground and defend himself from eventual disappointment, he imagines that the whole thing is a practical joke played at his expense by an unpleasant colleague, while at the same time taking the opportunity to explore the feverishly complex negotiation that is forever going on between the creative mind and the outside world.

Told of his good fortune, Samigli is blind to even the most obvious indications that he is being hoaxed. The idea that he is about to become an important literary figure is so much what he has always wanted to hear that every fact, however incongruous, is made to conform to his hopes. Brilliantly, hilariously, we are shown a patient, mild-mannered man turning into a monster of short-tempered vanity. The calamitous deterioration in his relationship with his invalid brother is particularly chilling, and when Samigli starts spending the money he hasn't yet earned, the story threatens to become seriously painful.

But this was not Svevo's way. If we compare him to two of his Italian contemporaries who also created anti-heroes with internal worlds in conflict with reality, one special and particularly happy characteristic of Svevo's work becomes obvious. In *Il piacere* [*The Child of Pleasure*] (1889), Gabriele

D'Annunzio created a Nietzschean superman who imposes his personal delirium on the world and above all on women with disastrous consequences. Luigi Pirandello, in *Il fu Mattia Pascal* [*The Late Mattia Pascal*] (1904), has a character who, yearning to escape society, takes advantage of his own supposed death to disappear and recreate an identity, only to discover that identity is not something that can be generated solely from within. However irritating they may have been, he needs the people who used to surround him in order to be himself. If he is not to be Mattia Pascal, the only thing he can be is the late Mattia Pascal.

D'Annunzio strikes the tragic note, Pirandello the tragicomic. But Svevo takes a different tack. Equally lacking in self-knowledge, equally unsure as to what would really be good for them, Svevo's characters somehow and against all the odds fall on their feet. So the hero of *La coscienza di Zeno* courts the elder of three sisters and is rejected; decides that the second is after all the one for him and is rejected; then ends up marrying the third, whom he had always thought of as plain and uninteresting, only now to find that actually she is the perfect wife, and, what's more, the one he really loves. It is a sort of comedy of complicity between various incomprehensions that, quite against all expectations and perhaps only in fiction, produces felicitous results. In this sense the fable of the man and the birds is telling: the man likes to believe they love him for the food; the birds enjoy the thought that they are outwitting his attempts to use food to catch them; so long as neither learns the truth, both are happy. What matters is the mental state, not the reality.

So the unfolding of *A Perfect Hoax* is a wonderful comedy where the resourcefulness of the vain and creative mind is aided by a variety of unlikely circumstances in its desperate effort to reconstruct self-esteem and serenity. The Italian title of the story, *Una burla riuscita*, is a little less specific than the English. It might simply be translated as 'a successful joke'. By the end of the story, however, the joke ceases to be just the hoax, or even Svevo's story, but becomes life itself.

– *Tim Parks, 2003*

INTRODUCTION

Italo Svevo's *A Perfect Hoax*, although a slighter work than the three long novels on which his reputation most firmly rests, is clearly cut from the same cloth. It is not difficult to trace autobiographical influences in the novels: in this shorter work I have the impression that Svevo went out of his way to stress its relation to his own life, almost as though he intended it to be read as a personal confession.

His pseudonym Italo Svevo (which translates literally as 'Italian Swabian', and mirrors his true Italian forename, Ettore, and German surname, Schmitz) to emphasise his dual background: his mother was Italian and his father of German descent. His protagonist in *A Perfect Hoax* has a purely Italian name, and (fortunately for his tormentor) knows almost no German. Nevertheless, the importance of Austria and the German language in his, and his author's, native city of Trieste is obvious throughout. More strikingly, the protagonist's surname, Samigli, was one that Svevo had already used as a pseudonym in his journalism; the choice of it here can hardly be an accident. Mario Samigli, like Svevo, is a literary man, involved also in the world of business, although it must be admitted with less success than Svevo. Literary success came to Svevo very late in life, as did Samigli's short-lived illusion of success. Svevo's enjoyment of his genuine success was also cut short, by his death in a car accident – an instance of what Oscar Wilde described as life imitating art and, strangely enough, something Svevo always feared. With Samigli, literary success seems to come bound up with translation, as it really did for Svevo; he made his name with his last novel, *La coscienza di Zeno*, and its success was initiated to a large extent by its translation into French.

It is significant that the translators of that novel into English have to begin by coping with the difficulties posed by the word '*coscienza*'. This means both consciousness and conscience, and there is no exact equivalent in English, so that the translator must be partly wrong whichever he chooses, or else be guilty of an evasion, by translating it as, say, *The Confessions of Zeno*. This is not irrelevant to *A Perfect Hoax*, because in this story, too, consciousness automatically implies conscience. The story is a study in psychology, but, for all Svevo's great interest in his contemporary Freud, the psychology is never a morally neutral matter of scientific cause and effect: the characters are seen as responsible for what they do, despite their remarkable ability to deceive themselves.

Some twenty years after Svevo's death, his friend, the poet Umberto Saba, mentions Svevo describing how, as a businessman before the First World War, he more or less strolled into a contract for the supply of an anti-corrosive underwater paint to the British Navy – in those days an almost unbelievably lucrative deal. Saba uses this as an example of how matters of great importance are often decided rapidly, while trivialities can take up time: 'It had taken five minutes for his precious underwater paint to be adopted by the most powerful fleet of warships in the world.' Saba mentions how Svevo had afterwards a vague feeling of guilt mixed with his elation. With that mixture of feelings, and that wholly unjustified, and yet all too human feeling of guilt, we are in the world of Mario Samigli.

The story's mixture of tones – from the solemn to the ludicrous, from the gentle and affectionate to the sheerly hateful, from the trivial to the impressive – is at one, of course, with the absurdity of the events. This absurdity includes what happens inside people's minds. As an instance, it is ridiculous that Samigli should be taken in by such a hoax, and yet all too believable also, for reasons which Svevo spells out later in the story. Similarly, the strange way in which he comes to realise he has been deceived (strange in the way the action unfolds, and strange in the way his mind responds) is not only believable but also uncomfortably, and comically, familiar to the reader. The story is not short on external incident, but it is the internal action which matters most.

This is why the objection that has sometimes been made to Svevo's work – that he deals with trivial matters in a provincial backwater – is quite beside the point. He clearly shies away from the grand and portentous, but this story is, in its own refreshingly gentle way, concerned with some of the outstanding themes of late-nineteenth- and twentieth-century literature. There is, for instance, the apparent opposition between the worlds of business and of art, or between the artist and the bourgeois world around him – an important theme in the last century; we need but mention Thomas Mann. There is also acute insight into the nature of the literary artist himself, and how he cannot help trying to transpose experience into an objective form: Mario Samigli is a mostly ineffectual writer, but he has the true artistic urges, and in fact his fables are, in their small way, quite effective. In his blundering way, too, Samigli does, despite his apparent ignorance of it, have a good intuition of how the literary market works.

It is not difficult for any writer to present us with absurd events. The trick is to present absurdities which are reminiscent of our own experience and therefore utterly believable. There are many such in this book: the relationship between Mario and his brother, which is based on a series of half-conscious pretences on both sides, and yet based very securely and affectionately; the strange, and yet perfectly natural way in which Mario unconsciously colludes in his own deception; the even stranger way in which he finally realises what he has, in some corner of his mind, known all along; and, the best example of all, the totally unexpected double denouement.

It is in this denouement that the story reaches its artistic perfection. The last thing we expect from Mario Samigli is physical violence, and yet we ought to have expected it. The incident also reveals something about ourselves if – as I must admit I do – we delight in the battering of Gaia. Unconsciously we have been hoping for something like this to happen, and the fact that Gaia is evil does not make our own reaction any more admirable. With the second denouement, the fulfilment of an ambition which Samigli did not have (commercial success) at the instant of finding that the success he hoped for is still eluding him – an achievement which comes by happy chance and the unselfish kindness of an uncomprehending friend – means that the cruelties along the way are ultimately subsumed into the benign, tolerant atmosphere which is the final impression the book leaves us with. As Saba noted, 'He was a nice man, old Schmitz!'

– *J.G. Nichols, 2003*

Note on the Text:
The current text is based on Italo Svevo, *Una burla riuscita*, Edizioni Studio Tesi, Pordenone (1993).

A Perfect Hoax

1

Mario Samigli was a man of letters, getting on for sixty years
old. A novel he had published forty years before might have
been considered dead if in this world things could die even
when they had never been alive. Mario, on the other hand,
faded and feeble as he was, went on living very gently for years
and years the kind of life made possible by the bit of a job he
had, which gave him very little trouble and a very small
income. Such a life is healthy, and it becomes healthier still
when, as happened with Mario, it is flavoured with some
beautiful dream. At his age he continued to think of himself as
destined for glory, not because of what he had done or hoped
to do, but because a profound inertia – the same inertia which
prevented any rebellion against his lot – held him back from
the effort of destroying a conviction formed in his mind so
many years before. And so in the end it became clear that even
the power of destiny has its limitations. Life had broken a few
of Mario's bones, but it had left intact his most important
organs – his self-respect, and even to some extent his respect
for others, on whom glory certainly depends. In his sad life
he was accompanied always by a feeling of satisfaction.

Few could suspect him of such presumption, because Mario
concealed it with the almost unconscious shrewdness of the
dreamer, which allows him to protect his dream from any
conflict with the hard facts of this world. Nevertheless, his
dream did at times become apparent, and then those who
liked him defended that harmless presumption of his, while
the others, when they heard Mario judging living and dead
authors decisively, and even citing himself as a precursor,
laughed, but gently, seeing him blush as even a sixty year old
can, when he is a man of letters and in that situation. And

laughter, too, is a healthy thing and not wicked. And so things went very well with all of them: with Mario, his friends and even his enemies.

Mario wrote very little. In fact, for a long time all he had which marked him out as a writer were the pen and the blank sheet of paper ready on his work desk. And those were his happiest years, so full of dreams and void of any troublesome experience, a splendid second childhood, preferable even to the maturity of the more fortunate writer who is able to pour himself out on paper, helped rather than hindered by the word, and who is then left like an empty husk which is nevertheless regarded as succulent fruit.

That era could only remain a happy one so long as he was making an effort to escape from it. As far as Mario was concerned, this effort, though not too violent, was always there. Fortunately he never found a route that would have taken him away from his great happiness. To write another novel like his old one, born out of admiration for the life of those who were superior to him in wealth and status, a life with which he had become acquainted using a telescope, was an impossible undertaking. He continued to love that novel of his because he could love it without a great effort, and it seemed alive to him, like anything which seems to have some rhyme and reason. But when he tried to set about working again on those shadowy people, in order to project them onto paper in the form of words, he experienced a healthy revulsion. The utter, although unconscious, maturity of sixty years prevented such an activity. And he did not think of describing more humble lives, his own life for instance, exemplary in its virtue, and so much the stronger through that resignation which controlled it, but was not vaunted and not even explicit, so much had it by now set its mark on his ego. He lacked the means and even the affection to be able to do that, which was a real drawback, but one common among those who were prevented from knowing any higher life. And he finished up by abandoning people and their lives, whether high or low, or at least he thought he had abandoned them, and dedicated himself, or so he thought, to animals, by writing fables. And so some very short and stiff little mummies (not corpses, because they did not even have a smell) were produced by him at odd moments. Childlike as he was (not through old age, because he had always been like this), he considered them a start, a useful exercise, an improvement, and he felt he was younger and happier than ever.

At first, repeating the error of his youth, he wrote about animals which he hardly knew, and his fables resounded with roars and bellows. Then he became more human, if we can put it that way, writing about animals with which he thought he was acquainted. So the fly presented him with a large number of fables, showing itself to be a more useful creature than one would have thought. In one of those fables he admired the speed of the dipterans, a speed which was wasted because it neither enabled the creatures to reach their prey nor guaranteed their own safety. Here the tortoise provided the moral. Another fable exalted the fly for destroying those filthy things which it loved so much. A third fable marvelled that the fly, the creature best endowed with eyes, had such imperfect sight. Finally, one fable told of a man who, after squashing a troublesome fly, cried out to it, 'I've done you a good turn. Look, you're not a fly any more.' With a system like this it was easy to have a fable ready every day with the morning coffee. It took the war to teach him that a fable could become an expression of his own mind, which inserted the little mummy into the structure of life, like one of its organs. And this is how that happened.

At the outbreak of the Italian war Mario was afraid that the first act of persecution that the Royal Police would carry out in Trieste would involve him – one of the few Italian men of letters remaining in the city – in a fine old trial which might send him to dangle on the gallows. This filled him with terror and at the same time with hope, making him now exult and now blanch with terror. He imagined that his judges, a full council of war, composed of representatives of the whole military hierarchy from the general down, must have read his novel, and – if there was any justice in the world – studied it. Then, without doubt, a rather distressing moment would arrive. But if the council of war was not composed of barbarians, one might hope that, having read the novel, they would spare his life as a reward. And so he wrote much during the war, shivering with hope and terror even more than an author who knows that there is a public waiting on his words in order to judge them. But out of prudence, he wrote only fables of doubtful meaning, and, between hope and fear, the little mummies came alive for him. The council of war could certainly not condemn him lightly for the fable which treated of a big, strong giant who fought on a marsh against creatures lighter on their feet than he was, and who perished, still victorious, in the mud which could not bear his weight. Who could prove that this was about Germany? And what reason was there to think of Germany in relation to that lion, which always won because it never went too far away from its own nice big den, until it was discovered that the nice big den lent itself to a smoking-out which was bound to succeed?

But in this way Mario got used to going through life accompanied always by fables, as if they were the pockets of his suit. A literary development he owed to the police, who, however, showed themselves to be quite ignorant of the local literature, and who, during the whole course of the war, left poor Mario in peace, disappointed and reassured.

Then there was a further small development in his work with the choice of more suitable protagonists. There were no longer elephants (such distant creatures), or flies with their eyes quite void of expression, but the dear little sparrows he enjoyed the luxury (a great luxury in Trieste in those days) of feeding in his courtyard with crumbs of bread. Every day he spent some time looking at them moving about, and that was the brightest part of the day, because it was the most literary, more literary perhaps than the fables which resulted from it. He wished he could kiss the things he wrote about! In the evening, on the neighbouring roofs and on a withered sapling in the courtyard, he heard the sparrows twittering, and he thought that, before turning their little heads right round in sleep, they were telling each other about the events of the day. In the morning there was the same lively and sonorous chattering. They must be talking about the dreams they had had during the night. Like himself, they were living between two experiences – real life and the life of dreams. In short, they were creatures with heads in which thoughts could nestle, and they had colours, attitudes, and even a weakness to arouse compassion, and wings to arouse envy, and so their own real true life. The fable still remained the little mummy stiffened with axioms and theorems, but at least it could be written with a smile.

And Mario's life became enriched with smiles. One day he wrote: 'My courtyard is small, but, with practice, one could throw away there ten kilograms of bread a day.' That was a true poet's dream. Where could one find in that period ten kilograms of bread for birds that had no coupons? Another day he wrote: 'I wish I could abolish the warfare on the little

7

horse chestnut in my courtyard in the evening, when the sparrows try to find the best place in which to spend the night, because it would be a good sign for the future of humanity.'

Mario covered the poor sparrows with enough ideas to hide their little limbs. His brother Giulio, who lived with him, professed to like his writings, but his liking did not extend to the birds in them. He claimed that they had no expressions. But Mario explained that they were themselves an expression of nature, and complementary to things that lie or walk, by being above them, like an accent on a word, a true musical sign.

The happiest expression of nature: in birds not even fear is pallid and despicable, as it is in men. And this is by no means because it is concealed by their feathers. It is in fact obvious, but it does not change their elegant organisms in any way. One ought rather to believe that their little brains do not ever experience it. The alarm comes from sight or hearing, and in its haste passes directly into the wings. What a fine thing it is to have a little brain void of fear in an organism in flight! One of the little fellows has been startled? They all fly off, but in a way which seems to say, 'This is the right time to be afraid.' They know no hesitation. It does not take much to fly when you have wings. And their flight is confident. They avoid obstacles by skimming them, and they go through the densest tangle of a tree's boughs without ever being held up or injured. They only start thinking when they are far away, and then they try to understand the reason for their flight, examining places and things. They bend their little heads gracefully to right and left, and wait patiently until they can return to the place from which they flew. If fear were involved in every flight, they would all be dead. And Mario suspected that they deliberately procured these moments of agitation for themselves. They could in fact eat the bread that was given to them in utter calm, and instead they close their cunning little eyes, and they are convinced that every mouthful is a theft. And this is precisely how they flavour dry bread. Like true thieves they do not eat the bread in the place where it has been thrown, and there is never any squabbling among them there, because it would be dangerous. The dispute over the crumbs breaks out in the place at which they arrive after their flight.

Thanks to such a great discovery, he drafted the fable with ease:

A generous man, regularly and for many years, had given breadcrumbs every day to some little birds, convinced that in their hearts they loved him for it. The fellow was blind, otherwise he would have realised that the birds thought him an idiot from whom, for years, they had been able to steal the bread without his managing to catch even one of them.

It seems impossible that a man who was always happy, like Mario, should have done such a thing as write this fable. Was his happiness, then, only skin-deep? To attribute so much malice and injustice to the happiest expression of nature! It was like destroying it. I also think that to imagine such dreadful ingratitude in birds was a grave offence to humanity, because if little birds that cannot speak speak like this, how would those endowed with long tongues express themselves?

And all his little mummies were at heart sad. During the war fewer horses passed along the roads of Trieste, and those there were were fed only on hay. And so there were on the roads none of those appetising seeds left intact by digestion. And Mario imagined himself asking his little friends, 'Are you at your last gasp?' And the little birds replied, 'No, but there is a shortage.'

9

Was it that Mario wished to accustom himself to thinking that his own lack of success in life was also a consequence of circumstances over which he had no control, so that he could accept it without repining? The fable remains a cheerful one only because anyone who reads it laughs. He laughs because that stupid bird does not remember the desperation to which on certain days it was so close, because it was not itself affected by it. But after he has laughed, he thinks of the impassive appearance of nature when it carries out its experiments, and he shudders.

Often his fables were dedicated to the disappointment which follows upon all human actions. Apparently he wished to console himself for his own absence from life by telling himself, 'I am fine doing nothing, because I do not fail.'

A rich gentleman loved the little birds so much that he dedicated to them one of his vast estates, where it was prohibited to trap them or even frighten them. He constructed fine, warm shelters for them for the winter, stocked with abundant food. After some time a number of birds of prey nested in the vast estate, together with cats and even large rodents which attacked the little birds. The rich gentleman wept, but was not cured of his kindness, which is an incurable disease, and he, who wanted to feed the little birds, could not deny food to the hawks and all the other creatures.

So this graceless mockery of human kindness, too, was thought up by the rosy-cheeked, smiling Mario. He cried out that human kindness only succeeds in nurturing life in any place for a short while before blood begins to flow in abundance, and he seemed happy with that.

And so Mario's days were always happy. One might even think that all his sadness passed into his bitter fables and so did not manage to cloud his face. But it appears that he was not so well satisfied during the night and in his dreams. Giulio, his brother, slept in a room next to his. Usually Giulio snored beatifically during his food's digestion, which in a gouty person can be irregular but is at least complete. However, when he was not sleeping, strange sounds came to him from Mario's room – deep sighs that seemed to arise from grief, and then intermittent loud cries of protest. Those loud cries echoed through the night, and they did not sound as if they could have come from the happy and gentle man to be seen in the light of day. Mario did not remember his own dreams and, satisfied with his deep sleep, believed he was as happy in his bed as he was throughout the working day. When Giulio, who was worried, told him about his strange sleeping habits, Mario thought that there was nothing more to it than a new system of snoring. But quite the contrary: given the regularity of the phenomenon, there is no doubt that those noises and cries were the sincere expression, in sleep, of a tormented mind. One might think that it was a manifestation which invalidated the perfect modern theory of dreams, according to which in repose there is always the blessedness of a dream of satisfied desire. But could one not also think that the true dream of a poet is that which he lives when he is wide awake, and that therefore Mario was right to laugh by day and weep by night? There is also another possible explanation supported by the above theory of dreams: there could in Mario's case be a desire satisfied in the free manifestation of his grief. He could, then, be throwing away, in his nightly dream, the heavy disguise which he had to wear during the day to hide his own presumption and be proclaiming, with sighs and shouts, 'I deserve more than this, I deserve something different.' An outburst which could also be safeguarding his rest.

The sun rose in the morning, and Giulio was always astonished to learn that Mario believed he had passed the night, so filled with sighs, in the company of some new fables. Quite harmless ones at times. They were worked out through several days. The war had introduced into the sparrows' courtyard a great novelty – shortage – and poor Mario had invented a method of making the scarce bread last longer. From time to time he appeared in the courtyard and renewed the sparrows' mistrust. They are sluggish creatures when they are not flying, and it takes a long time to rid them of their mistrust. Each of their souls is like a little pair of scales, one side of which is weighted by mistrust and the other by appetite. The latter is always growing but, if mistrust is also renewed, they do not bite. Strictly speaking, they could die of hunger in the presence of food. A sad experiment if taken to an extreme. But Mario only took it far enough to cause laughter, not tears. The fable (a little bird cried out to the man, 'Your bread would be tasty only if you were not there') remained a happy one too, because the sparrows did not get thinner during the war. Even at that period there were, on the roads of Trieste, abundant scraps on which they could feed themselves.

2

Mario's presumption harmed no one, and it would have been humane to leave him with it. Giulio nurtured it so well that with him Mario did not blush even when he realised he had revealed it. Indeed Giulio had understood it so well that he had adopted it more openly than Mario himself. He, too, when anyone else was present, did not allow himself to proclaim his faith in his brother's genius, but, without any effort, merely complied with what he saw done by Mario himself. And Mario smiled at his brother's admiration, not knowing that it was he himself who had taught it to him.

But he enjoyed it, and the room where the sick man passed his days between bed and Bath chair was a rare place in this world, because Mario found there a peace which he thought of as silence and concentration, while it was something which those more fortunate than himself find in places that are particularly noisy.

Full of glory as it was, that room contained little else. There was a light dining table which was moved from the centre of the room, where the two brothers had their breakfast, to the corner by the bed, where they dined. Giulio's bed had only recently been put into that dining room. Fuel was expensive during the war, and that was the warmest room in the house, so the invalid never left it during the winter. In the long winter evenings, in that room, the poet looked after the gouty man and the gouty man comforted the poet. The resemblance of this relationship to that of the lame man and the blind man is obvious.

By a strange chance the two old men, who had always been poor, did not have to suffer very greatly during the war, which was so hard on all the other inhabitants of Trieste. Their privations were diminished by the great sympathy which Mario had managed to inspire in a Slav from the countryside round about, which manifested itself in gifts of fruit, eggs and poultry. It is clear from this success of the Italian man of letters, who had never had any other success, that our literature prospers better abroad than at home. It is a pity

13

that Mario could not appreciate that success, which otherwise would have done him good. He accepted and ate the gifts readily, but it seemed to him that the peasant's generosity was owing to his ignorance and that success with the ignorant is often regarded as cheating. For that reason his heart was heavy, and to preserve his good humour and his appetite he had recourse to this fable:

A little bird was offered pieces of bread which were too large for his little beak. For several days the small bird picked at its prey to little result. It was still worse when the bread grew hard, because then the little bird had to abandon the refreshment offered to it. It flew away, thinking, 'The benefactor's ignorance is the beneficiary's misfortune.'

Only the moral of the fable fitted the peasant's situation exactly. The rest of it had been so much changed by inspiration that the peasant would not have recognised himself, and this was the main intention of the fable. It had been written to relieve the feelings, and it was not going to hurt the peasant, simply because he did not deserve that. And so, if one examines it carefully, one finds that this fable does display some gratitude, although not much.

The two brothers lived strictly regular lives. Their way of life was not disrupted even by the war, which threw the rest of the world into disorder. Giulio had been fighting successfully for years against the gout which threatened his heart. Going to bed early, and counting his mouthfuls of food, the old man said good-humouredly, 'I'd love to know whether, by keeping myself alive, I'm cheating life or cheating death.' This brother was not a man of letters, but one can see that, by repeating the same actions every day, one finishes up squeezing out of them all the wit that is in them. Therefore a regular way of life cannot be recommended too highly to the common man.

Giulio went to bed with the sun in winter, and long before it in the summer. He suffered less in his warm bed, and got out of it for a few hours every day, only in order to follow the doctor's advice. Dinner was served by his bed, and the two brothers ate it together. It was made more appetising by their great affection, an affection which dated back to their early youth. To Giulio, Mario was always very young, and to Mario, Giulio was always the older one who could advise him in every eventuality. Giulio did not realise how much Mario was coming to resemble him in his caution and his slowness, as if he too had gout, and Mario did not see that his elder brother could no longer advise him, and would never say anything that went against his own wishes. And that was the right thing to do. There was no question of advising or warning; what was needed was support and encouragement. That is also easier for a gouty person to do, although it may not seem so. And when Mario concluded the exposition of one of his ideas, or one of his hopes or intentions by saying, 'Don't you think so?' Giulio absolutely did think so, and agreed with total conviction. And so literature was a very good thing for both of them, and their frugal dinner was all the better, since it was flavoured with a gentle, firm affection which admitted no dissent.

There had been some dissension between the two brothers on account of those wretched little birds which carried off part of their bread. 'You could save one chap's life with that bread,' remarked Giulio. And Mario replied, 'But I make more than fifty birds happy with that bread.' And Giulio was immediately and irrevocably in agreement.

When supper was over, Giulio covered his head, his ears and his cheeks in his nightcap, and for half an hour Mario read some novel to him. At the sound of that pleasant fraternal voice, Giulio was soothed, his tired heart settled into a more regular beat, and his lungs distended. Sleep was not far away then, and, in fact, his breathing soon became louder. Then Mario lowered his voice, gradually and without any interruption, until he was silent. And then, having put out the light, he went away on tiptoe.

Thus literature was a good thing for Giulio, too; but one of its forms, criticism, upset him and threatened his health. All too often Mario would interrupt his reading to start a violent discussion of the value of the novel in question. His criticism was the grand criticism of the ill-starred author. It was his great release – it only *seemed* to trouble him – and it was his most splendid dream. But it had the disadvantage of preventing anyone else sleeping. Sudden remarks, sounds of disapproval, discussions with absent interlocutors, so many varied musical instruments alternating with each other and preventing sleep. And then, out of politeness, Giulio had to take care not to fall asleep, when every now and then he was asked for his opinion. He had to say, 'That's my opinion too.' He was so used to such words that, in order to pronounce them, he had only to breathe out through his lips. But anyone who is snoring cannot do even this.

One evening the sly invalid, who looked so innocent in his huge nightcap, made a discovery. In a troubled voice (perhaps because he was afraid of being found out) he asked Mario to read him his own novel. Mario felt the blood flowing more warmly into his heart. 'But you know it already,' he objected, while he immediately started to open the book, which was never far from him. The other replied that it was many a long year since he had read it, and he felt a real desire to hear it again.

In a pleasant, gentle, musical voice Mario began the reading of his novel, *One Man's Youth*, with the full agreement of Giulio, who started to let himself relax, murmuring, 'Beautiful, magnificent, very fine,' which made Mario's voice more and more warm and animated.

It was a surprise even to Mario. He had never read anything of his own aloud. How much more meaningful it became, enlivened by the sound, by the rhythm, and even by the shrewd pauses and the wise speedings up. Musicians – how lucky they are! – have performers who do nothing but study the way to present them in their grace and effectiveness. With writers, the over-hasty reader does not even murmur the words, and passes from sign to sign like a tardy traveller on a level road. 'How well I wrote!' thought Mario in admiration. He had read other people's prose quite differently and, in comparison, his own sparkled.

After a few pages, Giulio began to wheeze as he breathed. It was a sign that his lungs were beyond his conscious control. Mario, retiring into his own room, could not tear himself away from the novel which he went on reading aloud for a large part of the night. What a revelation that book was. It had stirred things up and gone into his mind and someone else's mind through the ear, our most intimate organ. And Mario felt that his ideas were returning to him renewed and embellished, and reaching his heart by new ways which it was itself creating. What fresh hope!

And the next day a fable was born with the following title: *The Surprising Success.* Here it is:

A rich gentleman had much bread at his disposal and amused himself breaking it up into bits for the little birds. But this gift benefited only ten or so sparrows, always the same ones, and much of the bread turned mouldy in the air. The poor gentleman suffered because of this, because nothing is so sickening as to see that one's gift is hardly welcome. But then he had the bad luck to be taken ill, and the little birds, who could no longer find the bread to which they were accustomed, twittered everywhere: 'The bread which was always there is no longer there, and that is an injustice, a betrayal.' Then a multitude of sparrows went to that place to marvel at the providence which had ceased to manifest itself there, and when the benefactor was well again, he did not have enough bread to satisfy all his guests.

It is difficult to discover the origins of a fable. Only the title reveals that this must have come to birth in the sick man's room, where Mario had had his success. No one who knows the ways by which inspiration works will be surprised that, from the simple success which Mario had achieved with his brother, he leapt ahead to that success of the poor chap in the fable, who had had to fall sick to achieve it. One may perhaps not understand the origin of those little birds which were malicious enough to complain in public but, through their avarice, kept their good fortune concealed from their companions, unless one supposes, which is rather difficult, that the poet, when he writes, is clairvoyant, and that in his own success Mario had had an intuition of Giulio's malice. Otherwise we need to believe that when a man in Mario's situation starts to analyse what success is, he attributes ill-will to everyone, even to the birds.

The following evening Mario had to be asked to continue the reading. 'You went to sleep too soon,' he said to his brother, 'and I'm afraid of boring you.' But Giulio had no intention of giving up the only literature which was quite immune from criticism. He protested that he did not fall asleep from boredom, which is in fact the enemy of sleep, but because of the sense of utter well-being which he derived from the pleasure of hearing certain sounds and thoughts.

And so what had started off in this way continued unchanged until the end of the war, and the war lasted so long that the novel – contrary to what had been asserted by the only critic who bothered with it – was too short. But this was no great difficulty for either Giulio or Mario. Giulio declared, 'I am so accustomed to your prose that it would be hard for me to endure any other kind, like something fiery or bombastic.' Mario was delighted and started again from the beginning, certain not to be bored. One's own prose is always the most suitable for one's own vocal organs. It's natural: one part of the organism speaks for the other part.

And Mario, going from success to success, showed himself all the more defenceless against the plot which was about to be hatched to harm him.

3

Mario had two old friends, of whom only one was about to be revealed as his bitterest enemy.

The friend who remained a friend until his death was his boss, a man not much older than he was, Signor Brauer. A close friend, because he did not act like a boss, but actually like a colleague. This relationship of equals had not arisen from an instinctive friendship or democratic convictions, but from the work itself which the two men had done together for years, and in which now one now the other was the superior. It is well known that even the most down-at-heel man of letters is more capable of writing a letter than someone who has never been soaked in literature. Brauer remained superior as long as it was a matter of understanding some piece of business, but he gave way to Mario when they had to put tenders down on paper or set out arguments. By this time the collaboration had become so effortless that the two employees were like two organs in the same structure. Mario was accustomed to guessing what Signor Brauer had in mind when he asked him to write a letter in such a way as to make something understood without saying it or to say it without making a commitment. Signor Brauer was always nearly satisfied, but never completely, and he often revised the whole letter, shifting Mario's words and phrases about, but keeping them unchanged out of blind respect. As he made these corrections, Signor Brauer became friendlier than ever, and excused himself, saying, 'You literary people have a rather too choice way of expressing yourselves. It won't do for common tradesmen.' And Mario was so little hurt by such criticism that he did his best to earn it: he put more preciosity into his letters than into his fables. And he was quick to recognise that the letter, as revised by Brauer, was more commercial than his, because that was the most certain way of not hearing any more talk of the letter, which bored him.

So many masterpieces composed in collaboration had created a very pleasant intimacy between the two friends. Each recognised the merits of the other. But there was something more: neither of them envied the other's superiority. In Brauer's opinion it was a great misfortune to be born a writer, and those who, through no fault of their own, had suffered such an accident, had a right to every protection from their more fortunate companions. And as for Mario, a head for business was precisely what he had never aspired to.

The only thing was that Mario was not entirely convinced that Brauer deserved a salary so much higher than his own. This envy was what it took to give birth to a fable. And so even poor Brauer was turned into a little sparrow, but he was accompanied in his metamorphosis by Mario himself. Bread was of course offered to the two sparrows, because they exist so that human kindness may be practised on the cheap. Brauer flew towards the bread by the shortest route, and therefore the lowest. Mario flew on high and that is how he came to arrive late. But he was happy to starve, being comforted by the beauty of the view which he had been able to enjoy from on high.

It must also be said that Mario was an excellent employee and that he never needed to be goaded into doing his duty. Besides those letters which he wrote in collaboration, he was responsible for much record-keeping and other inferior tasks which in business belong by right to men of letters who cannot do anything else. Even for these tasks, which Mario performed very conscientiously, Brauer was grateful to him, because he had therefore more time to direct the business, as was his desire and his duty. And so all the time he was becoming more shrewd, and the time was about to come when his commercial knowledge would be more useful to Mario than the latter's literature had ever been advantageous to him.

The other friend of Mario's, the one who was about to reveal himself as his enemy, was a certain Enrico Gaia, a travelling salesman. For a brief period in his youth he had tried to write poetry, and he had come into contact with Mario, but then the travelling with small bundle him had strangled the poet, while, in the inertia of his employment, Mario had continued living on literature, that is on dreams and on fables.

Being a travelling salesman is no job for an amateur. To

begin with, he spends his life far from a table, the only place where it is possible to write verse and prose; and on top of that, the travelling salesman runs, travels and talks – above all talks – until he is exhausted. It had perhaps not been difficult to suppress literature in Gaia. He had passed through that stage of idealism which also sometimes heralds the formation of a slave-driver, and there remained no more trace in him of that stage than there is of the larva in a winged insect. He could have been utterly pulverised, and then analysed, without one cell in his organism being discovered which was shaped for anything other than doing good business. Mario, a little unjustly, did not pardon him for such a radical transformation, and thought, 'Seeing a sparrow in a cage arouses compassion, but also anger. If one has let oneself be captured, that means that to some extent one belongs in a cage, and if, too, one has put up with it, that is a sure proof that one did not deserve any other destiny.'

However, Gaia was highly valued as a travelling salesman, something not to be despised, since a good travelling salesman is worth a fortune to his own family, to the firm which took him on, and even to the nation in which he was born. All his life he had gone round the little towns of Istria and Dalmatia, and he could boast that when he arrived in one of those towns, for one section of the population (his clients) the monotonous rhythm of provincial life was quickened. He always travelled in the company of inexhaustible chatter, appetite and thirst – in short the three social qualities *par excellence.* He loved a practical joke just like the ancient Tuscans, but he claimed that his jokes were more friendly than theirs. There was no small town through which he had passed where he had not appointed himself the one to play a trick. And so his clients remembered him even when he had gone away, because they went on being amused on the lines he had laid out.

This love of playing tricks may have been what was left of his suppressed artistic tendencies. And the practical joker is in fact an artist, a kind of caricaturist whose work is not made any easier by the fact that he does not have to labour, but rather to invent and lie in such a way that the victim becomes a caricature of himself. The joke has to be preceded and accompanied by a careful set-up, and of course a successful hoax becomes immortal. Certainly we talk more about one if it is related by a man like Shakespeare, but they say that even before him people were talking a lot about what Iago did.

It may also be the case that Gaia's other hoaxes were more innocuous than the one we are dealing with here. In Istria and Dalmatia his hoaxes must have been used to make money. But the trick he played on Mario was loaded with real hatred. Oh yes, indeed. He had a fierce hatred of his great friend. He may not have been quite conscious of it, because he was convinced rather that he felt nothing but a deep compassion for Mario, that wretch who was so presumptuous and had nothing in the world, stuck in a rotten job in which he could never get on. When he talked about Mario, he knew how to look compassionate, but he twisted his lips in a threatening way.

He envied him. Gaia was as much absorbed in bingeing as Mario was in fables. Mario was always smiling, and Gaia laughed a lot, but with interruptions. Fables always go with one like a luminous shadow by the side of that dark shadow cast by the body, while bingeing, when it casts a shadow, is atrocious. Because bingeing is an offence against one's own organism, and it is immediately followed (especially at a certain age) by the worst remorse of all, compared with which, that of Orestes, who killed his own mother, was very slight. With this remorse always goes the effort to alleviate it, explaining and excusing the offence, even asserting that it is the destiny of mankind to commit it. But how could Gaia proclaim in all good faith that everyone who could devoted himself to bingeing when there was always Mario?

Then there was that wretched literature. This, too, had the effect of troubling Gaia's soul, even though his soul appeared to be cleansed of it. It is not possible to go with impunity, even for the shortest space of time, through a dream of glory, without regretting it ever afterwards, and envying the person who preserves the dream even if he never achieves the glory. With Mario the dream oozed through every pore of that skin of his which was so quick to blush. The position in the republic of letters which had been denied to him he nevertheless claimed and occupied, almost in secret, but with no less right and with no restrictions. In fact he told everyone that he had written nothing for years (an exaggeration, because there were the bird stories), but no one believed him, and this was enough for the general consensus to be that he lived an elevated life, more elevated than everything around him.

And so he deserved envy and hatred. Enrico Gaia did not spare him his sarcasm, and at times he managed to get the better of him by talking about business matters and the economic position. But that was not enough for Gaia, because Mario himself enjoyed laughing at his own condition. Gaia would have loved to tear that happy dream out of his eyes, even at the cost of blinding him. When he saw him come into a café with that air of someone looking at things and people with the eternal, lively, serene curiosity of the writer, he said grimly, 'Here comes the great writer.' And Mario did indeed have the appearance and happiness of a great writer.

Gaia did not appear in the fables. However, one day Mario found out that little birds are most voracious: they daily devour so many of those crumbs that, put together, they would weigh as much as their whole bodies. And it had been difficult to find among the sparrows one which resembled Gaia – even if all of them recalled him in at least one respect. And in this resemblance Mario discovered the contradiction which later succeeded in rising to the height of a fable: 'He eats like a sparrow, but he does not fly.' And later: 'He does not fly – he is really lily-livered.' This certainly alludes to Gaia who one evening, after he had wounded a friend with his aspersions, had had to flee from the café, running like the wind.

4

The third of November 1918, a historic day for Trieste, turned out to be one that was scarcely suitable for a hoax.

At eight in the evening, at the request of his brother, who, from where he lay in bed, was panting for more news after hearing an account of the landing of the Italians, Mario went to the café to take that concoction sweetened with saccharine which the inhabitants of Trieste were in the habit of calling coffee.

The only acquaintance he found was Gaia, who was resting on a sofa, tired after being on his feet for an hour or two. I am sorry to say it, but it must be admitted that Gaia really looked like the spirit of evil. Yet he was not at all bad-looking. At fifty-five his white hair had a brilliance which reflected the light as if it were metallic, while the moustache which covered his thin lips was nevertheless dark. He was thin, not tall, and one might have thought him agile if he had not held himself rather crookedly, and if his little body had not been weighed down by the protuberance of a paunch which was both out of

25

proportion to the body and stuck out lower than is usual with men who owe them to inactivity and appetite alone, one of those paunches which the Germans, who understand such things, attribute to the effects of beer. His little black eyes were gleaming with cheerful malice and conceit. He had the hoarse voice of a boozer and at times he shouted, because he held it as axiomatic that he should speak rather louder than his interlocutor. He limped like Mephistopheles, but, unlike him, not always on the same leg, because his rheumatism attacked him sometimes on the right and sometimes on the left.

Mario was older than him, but, despite the fact that his hair was quite white (as is usual with serious people of his age), he was evidently fair, as could be seen all over his pink, serene, tranquil face.

Gaia became excited as he spoke of various events at which he had been present that afternoon. He became rhetorical, because the time had come to exaggerate his patriotism, which had not been very great before the arrival of the Italians. He knew how to exaggerate everything, that man, and was always ready to grow heated in favour of anything which pleased those who were, or could become, his clients.

Echoing at a distance, even Mario's words could be accused now of rhetoric. But it should be remembered that on that day words themselves – especially in the mouth of someone who had not been destined to take any physical action – were duty-bound to be strong and heroic. Mario tried to sharpen himself up in order to rise to the occasion and, naturally, remembered he was a man of letters. The most refined part of his nature was aroused to reach out to history. What he said literally was, 'I should like to be able to describe how I feel today.' Then, after a little hesitation, 'One would need a pen of gold to write the words on illuminated vellum.'

It was a renunciation, because, apart from anything else, there were at that time in Trieste no pens of gold and no illuminated vellum. But it seemed quite otherwise to Gaia, and he grew angry as only boozers can. He thought it an enormity that Samigli even dared to mention his own pen in the context of an event of historical importance. He tightened his lips as if to conceal some gross insult which was automatically taking shape in his mouth, then he opened out his fist, which had clenched of its own accord, while he looked at the pink nose of the man of letters. But he could not restrain a reaction, more efficacious than his words and even his fist, which he had been considering for a long time, but which still lacked the maturity which could only come from long preparation. The hoax was discharged onto poor Mario's head, like an explosive which had happened to come into contact with fire. This is how Gaia learnt that even a hoax, like any other work of art, can be improvised. He was not confident of success, and was prepared to call a halt to it after he had used it to show his scorn for such a presumptuous fellow. However, Mario took the bait so well that it would have required a great effort to free him from it. And Gaia let the hoax continue, bearing in mind that there were few amusements in Trieste. They needed to make up for too long a period of gravity.

He started off impetuously: 'I was forgetting to tell you. One forgets everything on a day like this. Do you know whom I've seen in the cheering crowd? The representative of Westermann Publishers of Vienna. I went up to make fun of him. He was applauding too, and he doesn't know a word of Italian. And instead of talking offence, he immediately spoke about you. He asked me what arrangements you had with your publisher for your old novel, *One Man's Youth*. If I'm not mistaken, you've sold that book?'

'Certainly not,' said Mario with some heat. 'It's mine, wholly mine. I paid the expenses of the publication down to the last penny, and I never had anything from the publisher at all.'

It looked as though the travelling salesman was attaching great importance to what he was hearing. He knew well enough what expression a man should put on when he suddenly sees the chance of doing some good business, because he used that expression at least once a day. He gathered his thoughts and bent forward as though he was about to start a race.

'Then there is the possibility of selling that novel!' he exclaimed. 'It's a pity I didn't know that. And what if they now throw that big German out of Trieste straight away? Then it's goodbye to the deal! To think that he came to Trieste just to negotiate with you!'

Mario was indignant, and it must be admitted with some surprise that indignation was the first feeling he had at the announcement of his unexpected success, while he had never felt indignation during the long years of waiting in vain. How could Gaia have thought that the novel was no longer his? Who had ever wanted to buy it in all those years? And he was overwhelmed by an anger which was unendurable because he saw straight away that he ought not to reveal it. He was now completely in Gaia's hands, and he saw that he must not offend him. But he realised to his grief that he was in the hands of someone whose thoughtlessness threatened to ruin him.

It should be remembered how upset and disorderly the world seemed to be in those days. If the publisher's representative had disappeared into the crowd, and was not himself thinking of reappearing, convinced as he was that the matter with which he had been charged had been concluded by someone else already, it would be impossible to track him down. The world had never seen a crowd like the one then moving between Trieste and Vienna, keeping to the few railway trains, or in the form of a continuous river, on foot, on the main roads, composed of the army in flight and members of the bourgeoisie emigrating or being repatriated, all anonymous and unknown, like crowds of animals driven along by fire or hunger.

He did not doubt for a minute the perfect truth of what Gaia had said. He was probably more disposed to believe it as a consequence of his novel's success every evening in his brother's room. And when, much later, he knew about the plot hatched to harm him, then, in order to excuse his own credulity to himself, he came up with the fable which says that many birds perished because two men lurked on the same spot, one of whom was good and generous, and the other wicked. On this spot there was, for a long time, bread from the former and, ultimately, birdlime from the latter. Exactly as advised in a worthless book in which we are told how to trap birds scientifically, and which, of course, we shall not name here.

Gaia exploited Mario's state of mind marvellously, since it was revealed to him so clearly. His only fault was to believe himself very astute. Really he was nothing more than a common hunter who knows the habits of his special prey. Perhaps I have exaggerated how astute he was. Before running off to find the all-important person, who was perhaps already leaving Trieste, he required from Mario a written statement which assured him of a commission of five per cent. Mario thought that was fair, but since they had to wait while the sluggish waiter found pen and paper, he proposed that Gaia should waste no time but go away immediately, while he would draw up the statement and send it to him the following

29

day. But Gaia did not want that. If they were to proceed safely, business matters could only be dealt with in one way. And the statement was drawn up with all care. In it, Mario committed himself and his heirs to pay the commission on any moneys which, now or in the future, were paid to him by Westermann Publishers. On his own initiative, Mario added to the statement an expression of gratitude which was nothing but a falsehood, because it had been suggested to him by his desire to conceal his two reasons for rancour. The first reason, the stronger, was the irresponsibility by which Gaia had compromised his interests, and the second, much less strong, was the distrust Gaia had shown by requiring that statement promptly.

Then Gaia, too, was in a hurry, and he rushed off. He could not wait to laugh openly. Mario wanted to rush off with him to shorten his own anxiety, but Gaia did not want that. First he had to go back to his own office, then rush off to a client from whom he might be able to get the German's address, and as a last resort he would go to a certain place to which the chaste Mario would certainly not agree to follow him, and where, without doubt, the German was to be found, if he was still in Trieste.

Before leaving him, he tried to cheer Mario up and prove to him that his own mistake was not very important. Now that he thought about it – he declared – he recalled that Westermann's representative had indeed been born into a German family, but in Istria. He would therefore become an Italian by birth, and could not be expelled.

This was the only action of his which showed his shrewdness as a trickster. Mario's great rancour had not escaped him, and he did not think that was the time to be provocative.

And so when Mario left the café he found himself out in the

dark night utterly and securely successful. He would not have felt like this if he had still feared that the German had been forced to leave Trieste. He breathed in deeply, and it seemed to him that never in his life had he breathed such air. He tried to repress the great agitation which troubled him, and he made every effort to think of the incident as something that was not at all extraordinary. Quite simply, he deserved it and it had happened to him – the most natural thing in the world. What was extraordinary was that it had not happened to him before. The whole history of literature was chock-full of men who were celebrated, and certainly not from their birth. At a certain point they had come across that really important critic (white beard, high forehead, penetrating eyes), or a wise business-man, a Gaia with qualities that made him more important than Brauer (who had grown too ponderous through his habit of dependence, and so could not play the part of someone who created business), and they immediately rose to fame. In fact, for fame to come, it is not enough for the writer to deserve it. What is needed is the combination of one or more other wills to influence those who are sluggish, those who then read what the first people have chosen. A slightly ridiculous process, but one that cannot be altered. And it can happen, too, that the critic may know nothing of another man's job, and the publisher (the man of business) nothing of his own, and the result is the same. When the two get together, then, even if he does not deserve it, the author is, for a greater or lesser period of time, successful.

It was very subtle of Mario to see things in that light, at that moment. Less subtly, when he added serenely, 'It's just as well that things are different in my case.'

Why hadn't the critic come to him rather than the business-man? He consoled himself by thinking that Westermann had surely been brought into that affair by the critic. And while the hoax lasted, he dreamed of such a critic, he built up his appearance and his character, and attributed to him so many virtues and so many defects as to make him larger than life. Certainly he was a critic who was not concerned at all with himself, and he was not in the least like other critics who, when they are reading, cast onto the page the shadow of their own shady noses. He did not talk idly, but acted, which was very strange for a man whose only action consisted in judging the efficacy of other people's words. He was more confident than critics usually are, because he was responsible for making only one mistake (a rather big one), and not so many as to fill several columns of a newspaper. What a great man! To be Westermann's aesthetic soul, his eye that never closed (because otherwise the publisher might find himself paying for false stones as though they were genuine, as Mario – who was no connoisseur – supposed could happen to jewellers). And so cold, like a machine that can only move in a single way. In his hands the work acquired its full value and no more, and became lifeless, like a piece of merchandise which goes through a middleman's hands, and leaves nothing in them but some financial profit. It did not make conquests, but was seized, weighed and measured, consigned to others and forgotten, so as not to hinder the operation of the machine that was immediately set in motion again. After reading Samigli's novel, the critic had gone to Westermann and said to him, 'This is a work which will suit you. I advise you to telegraph straight away to your representative in Trieste to buy it at any price.' Then he had done his duty. Would it have been too much for him to send Samigli a postcard to say those intelligent words which only he was capable of formulating? This, precisely this, was what the best critic in the world would have done. And to think it was worth the trouble of writing, if only because of the existence of such a creature!

And so it could be said that Gaia's hoax threatened to become very important, because right from the beginning it distorted the appearance of the world. And when Mario was forced to change his mind, he used a fable to take it out on none other than that critic he had himself created, the only critic whom he had liked:

A famished young sparrow happened one day to find many crumbs of bread. He believed he owed them to the generosity of the larger creature which he had never seen, a ponderous ox grazing in a field nearby. Then the ox was slaughtered, the bread no longer appeared, and the sparrow mourned his benefactor.

Such a fable was a true example of hatred. Turning oneself into a blind and stupid creature like that young sparrow merely in order to make the critic into such an uncouth creature!

So great did Mario consider his success that he took a decision whose result was to weaken the effect of the hoax. For the moment there was no need to tell anyone of his good fortune. When his book was published in German, the wonder throughout the city and the whole nation would be all the greater because it was unexpected. For Mario, who had waited for success for so many years, it would not be difficult to remain without it for a bit longer.

His brother, who was already in bed when he arrived home, began by voicing some doubt of the truth of Gaia's communication, but in an almost automatic sort of way, and the sort of doubt which comes to one at any surprising piece of news. But he was happy to banish straight away the last trace of doubt from his heart when he saw that it might lessen his brother's joy. He was not acquainted with Gaia, and so there was no basis for his doubt. Beneath his nightcap, his lively eyes shared all the jubilation. New things disturbed him and he did not think they were good for his health, but Mario's joy had to be his too. Ultimately, however, when Mario talked about their future wealth, he did not see it as important. It would not make his bed any warmer, and it would increase the temptation to eat those richer foods which menaced his health.

For Giulio even the first evening was much less pleasant than usual. Now that it had been brought back to life, the novel drew Mario's disquieting criticism. At every passage he read, he interrupted himself to say, 'Wouldn't it be better to say this in a different way?' And he proposed new words, asking Giulio to help him decide on them. Not in an argumentative way, but enough to take away from the reading its value as a lullaby. In replying to Mario's requests, Giulio opened his large, frightened eyes wide once or twice, as if he wanted to demonstrate that he was listening to the words addressed to him. Then he came up with an expedient which safe-guarded his sleep for that evening: 'It seems to me,' he murmured, 'that no change should be made in something that as it stands has succeeded. If you change it, perhaps Westermann won't want it any more.'

This expedient was as valuable as that other which had safeguarded his sleep for so many years. For that evening it served admirably. Mario left the room, but he was less attentive than usual, and he banged the door in such a way that the poor invalid jumped.

It seemed to Mario that Giulio was not supporting him as he should have done. Look how he was leaving him alone with his success still up in the air, more disquieting than a threat. He went to bed, but that evening the daze preceding sleep was terrible. He saw his success, in the person of Westermann's representative, dragged far, far away northwards, and killed off by the armed and infuriated mob. What an anxiety! He had to relight the lamp before he remembered that, even were his representative dead, Westermann remained, being nothing other than a joint-stock company not subject to physical death.

Once the lamp was lit, Mario cast around for a fable. He believed he had found one in the reproof he gave himself for not being able to enjoy in peace the promise of such good fortune. He said to the sparrows, 'You who do not provide at all for the future certainly know nothing of the future. And how do you manage to be happy if you're not waiting for something?' In fact he could not sleep for joy. But the little birds were better informed: 'We are the present,' they said, 'and are you really happier, living for the future?' Mario admitted that he had asked the wrong question, and he resolved to make another fable on a better occasion which would show his superiority over the little birds. With a fable you can get wherever you want, when you know what you want.

Brauer, to whom Mario recounted his adventure the following day, was surprised, but not excessively so: he knew of other merchandise that acquired value from one moment to the next, after being held in contempt not for a mere forty years, but for several centuries. He understood little about literature, but he knew that sometimes, although not very often, it was rewarded. He had only one fear: 'If you make your fortune with literature, you will end up leaving this office.'

Mario observed modestly that he did not think his novel

would make his living for him. 'However,' he added with a touch of pride, 'I shall ask to be given a position more suitable to my worth.' He was not really thinking of changing his position in that office, where the work was so easy, but men who are soaked in literature love to be able to say certain things. It is the most valued reward for their merit.

At that moment a letter was brought to him from Gaia, in which he was invited to be at the Café Tommaso on the dot of eleven. Westermann's representative had been found. Mario rushed away, not without having first asked Brauer not to divulge the news yet.

5

Gaia, Mario and Westermann's representative were all so punctual that they arrived at the door of the café together. They stayed there quite a while, as they made up quite a little Tower of Babel. Mario managed to say a few words in German to express his pleasure at making the acquaintance of the representative of such an important firm. The other, in German, said more, much more, and it was not all lost because Gaia translated assiduously: 'The honour of meeting... the honour of dealing... the famous work which his boss wanted to possess at all costs.'

Gaia also, acting boorishly rather than resolutely, said a few words which he immediately translated. He had declared that Westermann could have the novel when he had paid for it. This was a matter of business and not of literature. As he said these last words he smirked contemptuously, which was imprudent. Why abuse literature if it was true that it was being transformed here into a good business deal? But Gaia hit out at literature in order to hit out at the man of letters, forgetting that for the sake of the hoax he should preserve him in all his glory. And in the course of the conversation, Gaia remembered to say once to Mario, 'You keep silent because you know nothing.' Mario did not protest, certain that Gaia only meant he was ignorant of business matters.

Then Gaia was tired of standing in the open air. A fine, damp mist had gathered, destined to be swept away by the bora which was about to sadden those celebrated days. Gaia pushed open the door of the café and, without standing on ceremony, but allowing himself a burst of loud laughter, went in first, limping.

The other two were still waiting politely before going over the threshold, and Mario had a chance to study this most important person whom he was seeing for the first time. He was never to see him again, but he never forgot him. At first he recalled him as a very comical person, made even more ridiculous by the importance of the message with which he was entrusted. Then his memory of him did not alter much: he was still ridiculous, but his inferiority reflected badly on Mario himself, who had let the man walk all over him and treat him badly. Mario's wounds became more bitter when received at the hands of such a man. Mario could not be said to be a bad judge of character, but he was, unfortunately, a literary one, of the type that can be deceived with only the slightest effort, because their observation, although precise, is immediately distorted by the strength of their ideas. Now he is never without ideas who has any experience of this life, where the same lines and colours mark the most varied things, and only the man of letters is aware of them all.

The representative of Westermann Publishers was a shambling little fellow, without the air of authority conferred by a proportionate abundance of flesh and fat, but rendered ungainly by an excessive abdominal development noticeable even beneath his fur coat. So far he resembled Gaia. His fur coat, with its sumptuous collar made of sealskin, was the most important thing about the whole chap, much more important than the jacket and the torn trousers which were just about visible. His coat was never taken off; in fact it was buttoned up again immediately after it had had to be undone to allow access to an inside pocket. The high collar always encircled the little face furnished with a short beard and a sparse, tawny moustache under a completely bald head. And Mario noticed something else: the German kept himself so rigid inside the fur coat in which he was entombed that his every movement seemed angular.

He was uglier than Gaia, but to the man of letters it seemed a matter of course that he should resemble him. Why should the man who deals in books not resemble him who is concerned with wine? In the case of wine, too, something supremely refined had preceded and created the trade in it: the vineyard and the sun. As for the hauteur with which he wore that fur coat when out for a walk, seeing that it went well with an individual of the same species as Gaia, it was not difficult to understand why it had been adopted. Mario did not think for a moment that his keeping himself rigid was a way of suffocating an urgent need to laugh, but he recalled instead that rigidity was peculiar to that group of people, business agents, who want to appear something which they are not, and who, if they did not keep an eye on themselves, would betray their true nature. It cost Mario something of an effort to think like this. It was as though he were working to ensure the success of the hoax. He thought again that the critic of the House of Westermann had stayed at home, but that the great businessman, too, had stayed at home. Travel was not easy at that time, and it is clear that to conclude such a business deal it was enough to trust someone like that – a friend of Gaia's.

Around the table in the café, which was deserted at this hour, there was still something of a Tower of Babel. Westermann's agent tried to explain something in Italian and did not succeed. Gaia intervened: 'This man wants your express confirmation that I have the authority to deal on your behalf. I might be offended by his lack of trust, but I know that business is business. Although you're present here, he says he doesn't understand you.' Mario protested in Italian that what Gaia had arranged was binding on him. He said this pronouncing each syllable distinctly, and the German affirmed that he had understood and was content.

Gaia offered coffee, and immediately Westermann's representative drew from his breast pocket some large pieces of paper – the contract already prepared in duplicate. He laid it out on the table, and bent his whole chest over it. Mario wondered, 'Does he suffer from lumbago, too?'

Gaia was in a hurry. He snatched the papers away and started to translate the contract for Mario. He omitted those many clauses which were included in all the contracts of the great publishing firm, and spoke of all the advantages which he had procured for Mario with that contract. He used the very words which he would have employed if it had not been a bogus transaction: 'You will understand that I have earned my commission. I've spent the whole night in discussions with this man.' And he allowed himself to spit out a little of that venom he was full of: 'You wouldn't be able to do anything if I weren't helping.'

Westermann was obliged by the contract to pay Mario two

hundred thousand crowns, and in return he acquired the worldwide translation rights of the novel. 'In Italy you remain the owner. I thought to reserve this right for you, because who knows what value the novel may acquire in Italy when it is known to have been translated into every other language.' To make himself even clearer he repeated, 'Italy remains yours, completely.' And he did not laugh; his face was actually frozen in the expression of a man waiting for agreement and applause.

Mario thanked him profusely. He felt he was living in a dream. He would have liked to embrace Gaia, and not because he had made a gift of the whole of Italy to him, but because now he foresaw that in Italy as well, before long, his novel would win him his place in the sun. He reproved himself for the instinctive antipathy which he had always felt for Gaia, and he finished up by persuading himself of his affection: 'It's more than good, it's profitable. I gain by this, and it's very generous of you to be so pleased about it.'

He did, however, remember the anguish he had suffered overnight and, clutching Gaia's arm affectionately, proposed that a clause should be inserted in the contract obliging Westermann to publish the novel, at least in German, before the end of 1919. Poor Mario was in a hurry, and he would have been willing to sacrifice part of the two hundred thousand crowns, if by that means he had been able to hasten the advent of his great success. 'I'm not so young any more,' he said in apology, 'and I'd like to see my novel translated before I die.'

Gaia was indignant, and his contempt for Mario grew in proportion as Mario's affection for him increased. It really did take some presumption to argue about the offer which had been made to him for that utterly valueless apology for a novel!

Just as he had managed to conceal his laughter, so he

suppressed – and with the same effort – every manifestation of contempt. And for the chance of laughing louder later on, he would even have liked to find some way of inserting the clause Mario desired into the contract. But there was no room for it in those pages (actually devoted to a contract for the transport of wine in tank wagons), and also he could not possibly work in Mario's presence, or even pretend to work, when his whole body was ready to burst with laughter. Gaia, after a moment's hesitation – during which he was filled with so much malice that he felt himself constrained to cover his face with his hand to scratch, first of all his nose, then his forehead, and finally his chin (perhaps he could smile with one part of his face at a time) – solemnly started to discuss Mario's request. At first he voiced the doubt that Westermann might perhaps be annoyed by such great demands, and then, seeing that Mario looked upset at the denial of a request which would not harm Westermann at all, and which would give such peace of mind to him, Gaia had a brainwave: 'But don't you think that someone who has paid two hundred thousand crowns will have every reason to be in a hurry to make his money yield a profit?'

Mario conceded the force of the argument, but his desire was so strong that no argument could have got rid of it. Go on waiting? What would be done in all that time? Fables are only composed in days rich in surprises. Waiting is one adventure, or rather one misadventure, only, and it can provide only one fable, which he had already composed: the story of that sparrow which died of hunger waiting for bread where, by chance, it had been scattered once only (an example of greed allied with inertia, such as one comes across from time to time in fables). Mario hesitated. He tried and failed to find some other words (ones not too strong) to insist on his own request.

And so there was another pause in the negotiations. Gaia sipped his coffee while he waited for Mario's agreement, which wouldn't take long. Mario looked at the baldness of Westermann's representative, who was rereading the contract attentively. He had his long, pointed nose stuck in the contract, and the spectacles on his nose were trembling. Why were those spectacles trembling? Perhaps it was because that nose was going through the contract word by word, to see if Mario's desires were already satisfied there. The German's baldness, which was turned towards him like a face which was silent, blind, and without a nose, was very serious, because it lacked the organs necessary for laughter. In fact it was tragic – red skin sullied with some tawny hair. 'After all,' thought Mario, 'I shall be patient, and as soon as I have the money I shall be able to make my success public. It will be as though the book has already been translated.' He was resigned, and he prepared to sign the contract with the fountain pen which Gaia lent him.

Gaia stopped him: 'First the money, then the signature!' He talked excitedly with Westermann's representative, who immediately drew his wallet from his capacious breast pocket and stuck his nose into it to draw out a slip of paper which looked like a cheque. He gave it to Gaia, who made the mistake of looking into his face while he gave it. When two people are threatened by an attack of hilarity, it is essential that they do not look at each other. The two weaknesses add up and the pangs of laughter triumph. So it was a good policy to be stern; but Gaia, emboldened by the self-mastery which he had shown up till then, believed he was capable of another pretence – the anger which he showed as he spoke to the German of the need for immediate payment. The human organism is capable of every pretence, but not of more than one at a time. The weakness which came over him from trying to do that was such that he had to give way to an outburst of laughter which almost made him fall off his chair, and immediately, by contagion, Westermann's representative started to writhe in his fur coat. They laughed and they howled out rude remarks to each other in German. Mario looked on, trying in vain to smile to keep them company. Then he felt offended that a deal like that should be treated in such a way. The nobility of wine and of books was profaned by those unscrupulous businessmen.

At long last Gaia came to and took remedial measures. He drew from the German's wallet another piece of paper, very like that cheque indeed, and stammered through his laughter – which helped him now by giving him the time to think out an expedient which would explain it – that, instead of the cheque, the German had almost given him the receipt from a place mentioned the previous evening, where that swine went every day. And yet receipts like that are not to be found in such places. But Gaia had said the first thing that came into his mind, and to his great surprise that was enough for Samigli. 'The punishment for chastity,' Gaia thought then.

Mario was satisfied only because he was anxious to see everyone at the table serious again, and also to forget the unpleasant incident. The literary man's habit of deleting a phrase he regretted led him to accept easily such deletions when they were made by other people. The man of letters tells of reality, but he eliminates from it everything which does not conform to *his* reality. Here too he eliminated. He pretended, out of courtesy, to look at the receipt which Gaia was still holding up. He did it exactly as we look at a stranger who, accidentally, on a pavement, gets in our way for an instant.

This was how Mario signed the two copies of the contract.

43

Some days later, he was due to receive one back signed by the publisher. In the meantime, however, they were handing him the cheque which (as Gaia explained) was the equivalent of money – a draft from the firm of Westermann on a certain Bank of Vienna payable at sight on Mario's demand.

When they came out of the café, before leaving the German, Mario would have liked to thank him, and he tried to repeat in German a few words of thanks which Gaia had suggested to him. But then Gaia himself interrupted him: 'Don't bother. He's had his profit too.' He wanted to be alone with Mario, and he dismissed the other, who also seemed to be in a hurry to get away.

'Now,' suggested Gaia, 'let's go to the bank together to cash this cheque.'

Mario had nothing against the idea, but at that moment the clock in the square struck midday. Gaia regretted that he was late and was therefore unable to accompany Mario immediately to the bank, which was closing at that hour. 'Do you want to make an appointment for three o'clock?' He hesitated. In the afternoon he had another engagement, and he would be sorry to miss it. It would be distressing to sacrifice his own interests to a practical joke: if he did that, the joke would be on him.

Mario protested that he could get to the bank by himself. Had not he, too, been unfortunate enough to be engaged in business for many years? He suspected that Gaia was worried about his commission, and he reassured him: 'As soon as I get the money I shall bring you your ten thousand crowns.'

'It's not a question of that,' said Gaia, still hesitant. Then he made up his mind and explained: 'You shouldn't cash this cheque straight away. Westermann's representative asked me not to. It's signed by him, and with the post as it is these days, it's not certain that his advice will arrive in time.' Then he thought he saw Mario's face fall, and he added, 'But there's nothing to fear. If you look at the cheque you will see that it is signed by Westermann's proxy. You should deliver it to the bank, instructing them not to blacklist the signatory if the cheque is not honoured.' In the end Gaia seemed to regret his own words. 'I'm telling you all this mainly in order to avoid trouble for you. Even if you wanted it, as times are now the bank would not cash this cheque, even though it contains such a signature. And so it would be better to give it to the bank so that they can cash it. I'm not worried at all about my commission. I am as sure of it as if I already had it in my pocket.'

Mario promised to follow these instructions strictly. Besides, he had already thought of doing this. With that cheque in his pocket, he too was raised to the status of a businessman. And Gaia could be happy that the hoax would involve neither for him nor for Mario an encounter with the judicial authorities. There were also loftier reasons why his mind was at rest. He believed, that is, that all civilised countries recognised the right to perform practical jokes.

And Mario went on being blind. Gaia's disquiet had become obvious, but Mario did not notice it because at that moment he was tormented by remorse. Remorse is the speciality of the man of letters. It weighed heavily on him that he had always despised Gaia and was now receiving such a benefit at his hands. Up until then he had endured their friendship out of consideration for the memories of youth, which still prevail more than Gaia feel so strongly. Ought he not to make him feel that on that day the nature of their relationship was changing? On the other hand, he did not think he could do it immediately, because that would be like telling him that he wished to pay for his help not only with the commission but also with his friendship.

But Gaia, who was by now free of any disquiet, rushed away without waiting for the long-drawn-out decisions of the man of letters accustomed to the slow job of polishing. And, to clear away every cloud from his happy mind, Mario thought, 'When I give him the commission, I shall accompany it with a big kiss. It will be an effort, but I must be fair.'

Gaia had not foreseen everything. It turned out to be Brauer who went to the bank, at the request of Mario, who had had to stay in the office. Brauer followed conscientiously the instructions he had received: he delivered the cheque to go in the bank, and instructed that it should be returned to the payee without blacklisting the signatory if the cheque was not honoured. But the bank clerk, who was a friend of Brauer's, advised him to ensure for himself the rate of exchange on the day, and to Brauer, who knew the surprising rises in the exchange rate in those days, the excellence of the advice seemed so obvious that he followed it without feeling any need to ask for Mario's authorisation. Mario, therefore, together with the receipt for the cheque, had a counterfoil in which the bank declared it had bought from him two hundred thousand crowns at the price of seventy-five *lire* per hundred crowns to be handed over not later than December. Mario folded the two documents together and put them carefully into his drawer. Neither Mario nor Brauer realised that they had sold something which might not even exist. Brauer lamented that Westermann had not thought of it all two weeks before, because compared with that time Mario was losing fifty thousand *lire*. Mario smiled and shrugged his shoulders: a cut in his money was of no importance since the success was not being cut.

There was something else that Gaia had not foreseen. Some days later Brauer learnt of certain financial difficulties the two brothers faced, and persuaded Mario to accept a loan of three thousand crowns, because it was not right for him to suffer when so much money was already on its way to his address. That money was precious to Mario. He bought a host of things, each of which was a tangible sign of his success.

For a few evenings the two brothers gave up the readings, to admire the new furniture they had acquired, which sparkled among the faded furniture which had seen them come into the world. They also made a list of the objects they would buy when the money owed to Mario was paid. Everything at that time was very dear, but it seemed to Mario that his money had come very cheaply. Certainly, in the meantime, in addition to his success, the money, as well, had bought him great importance.

6

It was true that the time of waiting did not produce any fables, but in the long days that followed, entirely without event, Mario had to recognise that it was not monotonous, because not one of those days resembled the one that had preceded it or the one that followed it. Here is the story of some of them.

On several occasions Brauer went to the bank and, not finding the expected information there, he tried to persuade Mario to send a telegram to know quickly what had happened to his cheque. But Mario did not follow the businessman's advice, because he thought that here the practice of literature would be a hindrance. He knew from bitter experience how dangerous it was in literature to disturb one's patrons with reminders. At times he let himself be convinced that he should rush to the bank to send off that telegram, but then he was restrained by the terrible vision of an angry Westermann who might decide to do without the novel. A novel is different from all other merchandise. Mario thought that, if he were to lose that purchaser, he would have to wait a further forty years for another.

Besides, if he did decide to send that discourteous message (courtesy costs too much in a telegram), he would need to have Gaia's agreement. But that fellow was not to be found. Now that it was possible to move about, he had resumed his visits to his clients in nearby Istria. Mario gathered from one or two people that he had been seen in Trieste, but he did not manage to find him either at his home or in his office.

It was a very hard time. The money did not come from Vienna, and neither Westermann nor his adored, infamous critic turned up. Certainly the contracts and the cheque had been signed, but who knows if the ugly, fur-wrapped man had interpreted Westermann's wishes exactly. After all, that individual who could only speak German was no more than Gaia's translation into Italian. And so he could have been mistaken.

Mario had some experience of business and, it must be acknowledged, some experience of literature too. What he was utterly ignorant of was business in the field of literature. That was the sole reason why he did not manage to discover the hoax. If literature had not been concerned, he would never have supposed that such a practical businessman, as Westermann must be, would have offered so much money for something that he could have obtained very much more cheaply, for example for the small sum lent by Brauer. And now Mario owed that money, and he was no longer willing to admit that he would have surrendered the novel for nothing. But perhaps that is what is done in literary business, and editors must also have some of the humanity of patrons.

And Giulio, from his innocent bed, helped to dispel Mario's doubts. He said that Westermann, as he imagined him, must be a man for whom two hundred thousand crowns were more or less insignificant. And then what sense was there in verifying if there had been a mistake on the publisher's part? If that sly Gaia had tricked him into it, all the better.

Giulio's acute reflections were enough to make Mario happier for a few hours. Then he relapsed into the agitation of waiting. He found himself in a state which recalled the period following the publication of his novel. Then, too, the expectation of success – which had at first seemed to him just as assured as now the contract with Westermann was – had raged through his life, making it a torment which was unendurable even in memory. But at that time, given the strength of youth, expectation had not affected his sleep and his appetite. And although he had to believe that he was completely successful, poor Mario was learning that, after the age of sixty, he should no longer concern himself with literature, because it could become a practice that was very injurious to health.

He never suspected that he was the victim of a hoax, but certainly the more subtle part of his brain, that devoted to inspiration, unconscious and incapable of interfering in worldly matters except with the intention of laughing at them or bewailing them, admitted it. The following fable can be considered in some sense a prophecy:

In a suburban street in Trieste lived many sparrows, who fed happily on the many scraps which they found there. Then a rich gentleman settled there, whose greatest pleasure was to give them large quantities of bread. And the scraps were left on the road untouched. After some months (in the depths of winter) the rich gentleman died, and the rich heirs gave the sparrows not one crumb of bread more. And so almost all the neglected sparrows perished, since they could not return to their old habits. And in the suburb the dead benefactor was greatly blamed.

For some time, by means of clever expedients, Giulio had managed to safeguard his sleep. But one evening Mario unexpectedly interrupted the reading and ran for a dictionary to look up the meaning of a word. Giulio, violently brought back from that pleasant path that leads to sleep, along which he was sliding, came to his senses so thoroughly that he succeeded in defending himself with his customary guile. He murmured, 'For the German translation that doesn't matter.' But Mario, in whose soul the success was evolving, thought he ought to prepare also a second edition in Italian, and remained stuck in the dictionary. In fact, with the reverence which every good Italian writer has for that book, once he had taken it in hand he read a whole page. The reading of the dictionary was now like a motor car racing over a moor. And there was worse: on that page Mario found some indication that showed that at another point in the novel he had been mistaken in his use of an auxiliary verb. A mistake which he had committed to posterity! What grief! Mario, in his agitation, could not manage to find that point, and he asked for Giulio's help.

Giulio realised that the time had passed when shrewd expedients could protect him from literature, which had now become really unbearable. But he believed he knew from long experience that Mario would do anything he was asked to do for the sake of his health. And so he was touchingly sincere, but rather brusque, as anyone is who has been recalled from dreams to painful and boring reality.

He told Mario that it was his bedtime. In the morning he had to take some medicine, after which he had to rest for two hours before having his coffee. If he did not lie down immediately, what would the next day be like with all its meals shifted?

Mario experienced a feeling of contempt, quite different from the good-natured naivety with which, the week before, he would have accepted a disagreeable word from Giulio. He thought it his duty to feign indifference and hide his wound. He took up the book and the dictionary, and went out without remembering to shut the door. An appearance of indifference is gained at the price of increased rancour. As he went away he thought, 'Even with him it takes my success to make him respect me more.'

And Giulio, close to the door which remained open, spent a horrible night. Because of the bora, the squeaking of the hinges of the door onto the corridor was added to the noise made by the shutters in the room. And the invalid felt as if he had spent the night in a dictionary echoing with words in alphabetical order, rising to a startling, unexpected scream.

The next evening, after supper, Mario stayed with his brother and, once the table was cleared, he went off without having said a word to hint at his resentment. He had even helped his brother to serve himself. He felt that he had done his duty and had conceded everything to his brother which he had to. He was quite decided not to do more. So Giulio did not want the dictionary which he so urgently needed! Then if he wanted the reading, he would have to have it alone. It was without any remorse that he learnt that, by his own negligence, he had spoilt his brother's sleep. What did it matter? Did he not sleep better perhaps with those dreams of Westermann and his representatives?

But Giulio felt an urgent need to make peace. Mario, who had now turned taciturn, did not any longer even give him the city news, which Giulio awaited as one of the most valid reasons for living. He was the elder, but seeing that the other was the one who had been offended, with the weakness that accompanies illness, he decided to take the first step. In his solitude he thought it over for a whole day, and perhaps he was so mistaken because he had reflected on it too much. Or it is more likely that, after such a long period for reflection, one ends up with too clear an idea of one's own rights and one's own misfortune, which certainly does not help to make one more wary.

He addressed Mario as his brother, confiding to him what he needed for his own life, that is his own care. Among other things he needed a gentle reading, calling up pleasant imaginings and nursing his tortured organism. Why could they not go back to their old authors, De Amicis and Fogazzaro?

It is strange to find such naivety in a weak invalid in such need of cunning. Had he, then, forgotten the outcome, so happy, of his contrivance of some years ago, when he had proposed to abandon De Amicis and Fogazzaro and put his brother's work in their place? Yes, in contrast to the sparrows, a man, when compelled by a need, will expose himself to any risk to satisfy it.

Mario had to restrain himself from giving a start when he heard that the two lucky writers were about to supplant him even in that one little corner of the earth which had up till then been all his own. To think that, at the very moment when the whole world was being opened up to his success, he was being given a final kick from those who had always rejected him! To that end they were even making use of the ankylosed foot of that imbecile brother of his, who by this action definitely put himself on the side of his enemies.

It was hard for him to feign indifference, and his voice trembled with indignation as he declared to his brother that for some time reading aloud had been an effort for him, and that for the sake of his throat he should not do it any more.

Giulio took fright, because he realised immediately the mistake he had made, and he understood Mario completely. It was a terrifying prospect for him to see his solitude prolonged even into the hours of evening, when he was more in need of affection than of the reading which helped him to sleep. He tried to correct his error, without delay: 'If you want, let's go back to your novel. I agree completely. I only wanted to spare myself that dictionary: it's hard to endure the reading of it.'

Poor Giulio did not know that there is only one way of mitigating an involuntary offence: pretend not to realise it and to believe that the other had not understood it. Any other explanation is the same as confirming it, renewing it.

And Mario, cut to the quick, cried out, 'But haven't I told you about my throat? For this, the prose of Fogazzaro, or De Amicis, or my own amount to the same thing.'

It was a downright lie, but Giulio was not shrewd enough to realise that. He said mildly, 'You know that I love your prose more than anyone else's. Have I not been listening to it every evening for so many years, even though I know it almost by heart? It's only the corrections which bore me. We who are not men of letters like things to be definitive. If in our presence only a word is changed, we disbelieve the whole page.'

The invalid had shown signs of a certain critical talent, but at the same time of a boundless naivety. Had he, then, made Mario read to him things that he already had by heart? Was that not a dreadful rebuke? Mario's anger overflowed, and once he had let it burst out he was himself pervaded by it, as always happens with men of letters to whom words are not an outlet but a stimulation. He exclaimed, putting into his voice all the scorn he could, 'You make the same face at literature as when you swallow your salicylic acid. It's downright offensive. It's reasonable to concentrate on being cured, but not beyond a certain point. One's own life cannot be so important that, in order to prolong it, it is worth transforming all the most noble things on this earth into clysters.'

Literature, once it was attacked, had reacted by offending illness. Deeply. Giulio tried to find some words, but he could not even get his breath. Mario closed the door as he went out, but the invalid had a sleepless night, because he spent it in the first place in trying to convince himself that it was not his fault he was ill (which was difficult, seeing that his doctor was always asserting that the illness came from a mistaken way of life and the wrong diet) and then in getting angry with Mario, who, by scorning the treatment he was forced to take, gave an indication of wanting him dead. But he did not spend the entire night in discussions with his absent brother. He realised more than ever the uselessness of his life. Now he understood quite clearly that, by living, it was not death he cheated but life, which did not want to know about ruins like him who served no purpose. And he was profoundly grieved at this.

Mario did feel some hesitation, and even some remorse, before he had finished his diatribe. But he did go on to finish it, even rounding it off by spitting out that spiteful remark about treatments, in which he took the clyster as their emblem. He finished it even though he saw the imploring look in Giulio's eyes, and Giulio's weakness in seeing himself attacked at the core of his being. But Mario was composing. In devising that imaginary clyster he had the same satisfaction as in composing a fable.

Shortly afterwards, in the solitude of his room, Mario's satisfaction diminished. All compositions become boring eventually, and already that clyster did not seem to him such a wonderful thing. However, he was still angry, like an offended Napoleon – literature, too, has its Napoleons. Was it not Giulio's duty to help him in his work? And for the time being Mario ended up feeling sorry for himself. He had to put up with it all, he did: and aside from everything else, even Giulio's brutality and remorse for having offended him.

However, in spite of being so angry and feeling himself far superior to the invalid, and without much conviction of his own wrongdoing, he would willingly have gone to Giulio to ask for his pardon. But he felt that he would not make full amends by his words alone, which were bound to contain some rebukes in defence of his own dignity. It takes much more than words to heal the wounds produced by words. Because it was true that Giulio's life was not worth living, and he who had said it to him had revealed a truth that could no longer be denied or forgotten. Things left unsaid are less obviously alive than those which have been pointed out by words; but once they have acquired this life they cannot be diminished by other words alone. And Mario calmed himself down by his intention of renewing his old affectionate relationship with his brother when his great success was known to everyone. By that time his words would surely suffice to have some effect.

This was the intention to which he adhered strictly, and he did not realise that it would have been better not to wait for the arrival of the tardy Westermann before making peace with the invalid.

Giulio was indeed suffering. Even when Mario went back to being affable and talkative, he could not forget how he had been offended. First of all there had not been those explanations which feeble people, especially (since they love words so much), expect as a means of making up every difference, and then they had not gone back to their dear old habit of reading in the evening. Yet he was frightened of explanations, simply because he had already shown himself so weak in them. And in order to have them without having to speak, he thought of substituting energetic action for words: ostentatiously he stopped taking his treatment and hoped that Mario would be aware of this and be sorry. Instead, Mario did not notice anything, perhaps because the demonstration did not last long enough. The invalid had immediately felt himself getting worse and, taking fright, he had returned to his treatment, which, however, did him less good. How can a medicine act beneficially when it has been so scorned?

And so it was that Giulio, incapable of action, went back to words, which, however, he devoted solely to the action which he had attempted and not completed. One evening, with a gentle smile and without looking his brother in the face, he said, as he interrupted their supper to take certain powders, 'Against all reason I keep on with my treatment, as you can see.'

Mario, who, like the great man that he felt himself to be, attached less importance to their dispute, of which no trace remained but the great convenience of not giving the evening readings, was amazed, and loudly proclaimed that it was Giulio's duty to look after himself in order to get better, as if he had not in an even louder voice said the opposite a few days previously.

That was too little to pacify Giulio. Mario did not notice it.

He was merely amused to observe that Giulio looked like an obstinate child as he gulped down the powder dissolved in water. He seemed to be saying, 'I am looking after myself. I have the right to look after myself, and I have also the duty to do it.'

For a man of letters one attitude is enough to construct a whole person with the limbs needed to strike such an attitude and also other useful features. He constructs this personage, but he does not believe in it, and he loves it particularly if he can believe it to be one of his own imaginings which can nevertheless move about on the real earth and be lit up by the everyday sunlight. And if such a construct really does exist, he is not even aware of it, because it has no relevance to his concept. And Mario, in order to give his imaginary character a plausibly obstinate expression, substituted for Giulio (who he did not think even remembered his words) a stronger character (but one that was just as ill), proclaiming his right to live, exactly as he did in his warm bed, and to be helped by medicines and also by readings, as he wished. And Mario loved his own creation – that feebleness, and that obstinacy, and such great resignation. That foreshortened figure was an illustration of a life that was poor and full of suffering, but still capable of safeguarding such great poverty and grief.

It takes an effort to form a construct rather than look at what already exists. But it sufficed to illuminate his relationship with his brother. Because, as soon as he had created that figure, Mario looked around, as literary people do, to surround it with friends who would set it in relief, and in the midst of whom it could live. In the first place, of course, he hunted closest to his brother, whom he believed he had himself restored to health, by correcting him. But when one is dealing with oneself one is not so easily mistaken, and straight away one cuts into living flesh. He realised that he was lucky that Giulio was not up to judging him, because he, the successful man, had acted in a way of which he should be ashamed. Really disgracefully. He had tried to wound and upset the poor invalid whom destiny had entrusted to him, simply because he had, in all innocence and once only, rejected his work. He was by now nothing more than 'a successful man', someone in whom ambition had been twisted into a ridiculous vanity, and who believed that the usual laws of justice and humanity did not apply to him. He looked back into the not-so-distant past at his gentle, spotless life, devoted with utter unselfishness to one ideal, and he envied it and lamented its loss.

Now and then, for just a moment, the ideal which exalted him did reappear. But then the durability of an elevated ideal is irrelevant, because if it has existed, it will remain, and never be forgotten. In the future Mario was to find comfort and take pride in it. Always glimpsed rather than embraced, that ideal evolved, when it was not immediately rejected and negated by a passionate desire for the happiness which success gives. One day Mario felt his heart sink when he noticed that success had destroyed his love of fables. For days he had not produced any or even dreamed of any. His success had attached his ideal to the ancient novel, which he was examining in order to revise it, to adorn it, swelling it with new colours, new words. Success was a golden cage. Westermann had said what was wanted from him and he had been ready to give what he was asked for and nothing else. Later, when the hoax had been revealed, he began to return to his old life with the fable in which he told of a singing bird in a cage, which was proud of singing about nature but could only talk of the bowl of water and the bowl of millet between which it lived. And it was a great comfort to him to find himself ready to reject (as he then had to) the ridiculous notion that he deserved applause and admiration, and ready to accept the destiny imposed on him, as something human and not despicable.

But at first, not even during those brief instants of enlightenment, did he ever think of rejecting the success which was offered. In vain did the voice of Epicurus, rendered faint by its distance in time, preach, 'Live in obscurity!' He panted for renown, like all those who believe they can attain it, and he was sick of the long, vain wait.

7

Gaia was surprised and annoyed that Mario did not broadcast the hoax himself. Gaia was not broadcasting it in order not to compromise himself further, and also because he believed there would be no need. He had instead waited to see it given publicity in some local papers by some of Mario's friends. What kind of author was Mario if he did not rush through the city to broadcast his success? Busier and busier, Gaia did not find the time to approach Mario and make him chatter and enjoy it. And the hoax which was so late in bearing its fruit remained for him always a noble one, a promise of the joy which he deserved.

One evening, having returned from a tiring journey in a carriage on the small, slow, and therefore long Istrian railway, he stopped for some hours at an inn in company with some friends. And as the wine made him forget how stuffy the carriage had been, he recalled the hoax to take his mind off some irritating business matters. He recounted it, and then he had an idea which entranced him. He suggested that one of those present, who knew the Samigli brothers, should go to Mario and propose, on behalf of another German publisher, to buy the book at a price higher even than that offered by Westermann, and with a contract that obliged the publisher to publish the novel immediately. He burst into laughter at the thought of Mario's regret at finding himself already committed to Westermann.

Those present thought the hoax was wicked and refused to go along with it, and Gaia renounced it, and made them promise to say nothing to the two brothers of what they had talked about that evening.

Then he did not think any more about it, which was for him the easiest thing in the world. The first hoax had given him much amusement, and he stood to derive yet more pleasure from it, if from nothing else, from being present at Mario's grief, and perhaps also from what he termed his recovery from all his presumption. It seemed an easy thing to him to avoid being reproached by anyone. Westermann's representative was only a travelling salesman who had touted in Trieste when Austria had been defeated there, condemning him to idleness and disposing him to take part in a light-hearted hoax. He was by now far away from Trieste, and Gaia could declare that he, too, had been taken in by the hoax. He supposed that even Mario might be spirited enough to laugh at the hoax. That was not very probable, since people who love glory cannot laugh, but if Mario were able to rise to such a height, he could become his worthy companion, and would be able to drink with him in all friendship.

But meanwhile he had been very imprudent. One of those friends of his maintained his silence with everyone except his own family, and one of his little boys, whom he sent to the Samigli brothers from time to time to ask after them, reported to Giulio roughly what he had learnt. He said that Gaia had tricked Mario by making him believe that an actor-manager called Josterman had undertaken to put on one of his comedies. The whole thing was so garbled that Giulio thought at first it was about something else and did not concern Mario.

Mario, too, laughed about it to start with. The two brothers were having supper together and it was surprising how, after they had eaten a few mouthfuls in complete calm, Mario all of a sudden, by himself, without anyone having said another word, felt he was actually about to die, as he realised the whole of the hoax. He realised it with enormous surprise, and at the same time he was surprised that he had had to wait for a vague word of warning to know it all. Had he closed his eyes deliberately so as not to see and understand? Right from the start he had guessed the true nature of the two gentlemen he was dealing with, and he could have exposed them straight away when in his presence the two brazen-faced fellows had given themselves up to laughter. Why had he not thought? Why had he not looked? He remembered something else: the spectacles on the German's thin nose had trembled with suppressed laughter – an oscillation like that of a motor-car engine. By then Mario's thoughts were quick and sharp enough to discover something which had been clearly perceived by his eyes but not until then communicated to his brain: that scrap of paper taken by the German from his wallet, and which provided an excuse for the laughter to which the two cronies had abandoned themselves, was covered in Gothic capitals. Gothic, all straight lines and angles. He was as sure of it as if he were still reading it. And so it could not have come from a brothel in Trieste. Liars! And liars who had signalled their contempt for him by not bothering even to be on their guard.

61

If he had been mocked, he deserved to be punished. And he wanted to punish himself immediately by biting his lips. But such clear-sightedness was nevertheless accompanied by doubt. A further demonstration of his own incurable stupidity? Poor Mario! However obvious something may be, when it brings so much grief, it is never accepted without some attempt to obscure it. Everyone fights against his destiny as well as he can, and Mario tried to arrest his by telling himself that he was not obliged to admit it was a hoax before he had discovered its purpose. For the pleasure of laughing? But that is a pleasure which the one who is laughed at does not understand.

However, he tried to free himself from the doubt not because it seemed to him ill-founded, but because he thought it contributed to his agitation and increased his grief. He wanted to pass the night in certainty. And there was no other way to gain certainty than by reflection. Outside, the bora was blowing, lowing and howling, and if that had not been enough to restrain Mario, there was also the impossibility of catching up with Gaia, who was impossible to find, especially at night.

Meanwhile he had to know precisely what the little boy, their friend, had said. And so he began a close interrogation of poor Giulio, who did not remember the words, not having attached much importance to them. And the sick man could not endure Mario's frown. He had already suffered greatly, realising what was happening to his brother, right then, in front of him, but now he suffered still more in the fear of seeing himself rebuked again for his own weakness, his own life. It ended up with a few tears rolling down his emaciated cheeks.

At the sight of such signs of grief from his brother, Mario

became even more agitated. To grieve over the hoax in that way was to recognise that one had been beaten and to attribute a great importance to the hoax. He shouted out, 'Why are you weeping? Don't you see that I, whom the thing concerns so much more directly, am not weeping at all? And you will never see me weep. On the contrary, I live in hopes of making Gaia weep if he truly has hoaxed me.'

He could not bear Giulio's weakness. He abandoned his supper and, quickly taking his leave of Giulio (against whom he actually did bear some rancour for not remembering properly what their friend the boy had said), he withdrew to his own room.

And once he was alone, he felt he was certain and had eliminated every doubt definitively. The hoax had the same intention as all those which Gaia had strewn over Istria and Dalmatia, and which Mario now recalled he had heartily laughed at. Yes! One laughed at a hoax, and that was it. Everyone laughed who was not forced to weep. And, remembering this, Mario wept all at once, according to the laws of the hoax.

Without undressing, he threw himself down on the bed. He kept on hearing the burst of laughter the two conspirators had given themselves up to in his presence. It re-echoed throughout the incoherent noise of the bora, and there it became enormous. It struck at all the dreams that had embellished his life. If Gaia had wanted this, for an instant he had gained his object: Mario was ashamed of his own dreams. The hoax could not fail, however crudely it was devised. The hoaxer's clever work had preceded it, and did not need to accompany it. The hoaxer had spied upon him, and had presented him with a contract which had not been invented but copied from his mind. Had he not been waiting for something like this for half a century? And when it came to him, he was not surprised, or even mistrustful. He had not even looked into the face of those who brought it to him. It was something that was due to him, and it came to him by a certain way that had no importance. And so he had been tricked just like cuckolds and imbeciles in other ages, people who deserved to be tricked.

This, and not the loss of the promised money, was why the hoax rankled with him. Not for an instant did he think of the debt he had contracted with Brauer in consequence of the hoax. First of all, the things they had bought were still untouched in the house, and besides it is impossible to imagine what commitments can be fulfilled through honest work. The money was not important. What did torment him was the conviction that he had lost for ever his reason for living. Never again would he be allowed to return to the state in which he had always lived, feeding on the usual scraps seasoned by that lofty dream which set a permanent smile on his lips.

The adjective 'hoaxed' only really suits someone who lives in a city which is too small for him to walk through its streets safely, that is, unrecognised. All his familiar weaknesses accompany him along with his shadow. All the people of the same class as him know each other and all dig their claws into their neighbours' wounds. Each of us has his own fate down here, but when everyone knows what it is, it is made harsher by one meeting, by one glance. He would never be free of the brand that this hoax had set upon him, though he had been able to forget a woman who had once tricked him with a refusal. She was old now, but she still could not repress a malicious smile when she saw him. With the impartiality of the man of letters, Mario remembered also that he was a living reproof for someone else, since there was in the city someone who became agitated at the mere sight of him. Being a kind man, he had tried to improve that relationship, but had not succeeded, simply because such embarrassments are not removed, but aggravated rather, by explanations. And he had never played hoaxes, but life could devise ones much more atrocious even than Gaia's, and one merely had to know of them to be considered a true enemy by their victims.

That night would have been dreadful if fables had not intervened to lighten it. They turned up innocently, as if the incident with Westermann did not concern them, and they found immediate and unopposed access to that room. They deserved such a welcome. They were quite pure, not sullied by the hoax. No one had ever seen them. They were purer still because Mario himself had never considered them as anything but an appendix to himself, one of his ways of smiling and breathing. Gaia had not foreseen that, while he might cure Mario of one kind of literature, he could not cure him of all literature.

There were three of these kind comforters and they went hand in hand, but each of them revealed itself distinctly at the opportune moment to console him and guide him.

This is how the first revealed itself. Mario shuddered at the thought that he would not be man enough to punish Gaia, not because he was afraid of him, but because he would not be able to accost him and face the derision he deserved. A little bird near to him sighed: 'Even weakness brings its comfort.' And this fable was born:

A little bird was choked by a sparrowhawk. It was only given enough time for a very brief protest, a single, very loud cry of indignation. It seemed to the little bird that it had done

65

the whole of its duty, and its little soul was proud of that, and flew in its splendour towards the sun, to be lost in the azure sky.

What a comfort! Mario paused to admire that azure sky to which the souls of little birds belong as ours do to paradise.

The second comforter came to correct with a smile his loudly announced intention of not concerning himself any more with literature. That intention had come to him very late on. And Mario was able to laugh at it as if some innocent little creatures near him had committed the same mistake:

A little bird was wounded by a shot from a gun. His last efforts were devoted to taking flight from the place where he had been struck by such a din. He managed to get himself into the obscurity of the wood, where he breathed his last, murmuring, 'I am saved.'

And the third comforter clarified what the second had said. Because to hide one's own love of literature is easy. It was only necessary to beware of flatterers and publishers. But to renounce literature? And how could one live then? The following tragedy encouraged him not to do what Gaia wanted:

A little bird, blinded by its appetite, let itself be caught with birdlime. It was placed into a horrible cage where it could not even spread its wings. It suffered dreadfully, until one day its cage was left open, and it was once more at liberty. But it did not enjoy it for long. Experience had made it mistrustful, and where it saw food it suspected a trap and fled away. And so in a short time it died of hunger.

And, comforted by those three little birds, which had all died, Mario might even have been able to sleep, but he noticed then that his room lacked something to which he was accustomed: his brother's snoring. Hadn't Giulio gone to sleep yet? At that late hour! That would be a serious matter.

On tiptoe he approached the door into the other room. The light there had gone out, but Giulio, who was still awake, heard him and asked him to come in.

When Mario had lit the lamp, Giulio looked at him timidly and, afraid that he was going to have to endure further rebukes, he confessed his own perturbation: 'I can't get over the fact that I've saddened you by not being able to remember the exact words which that little boy said to me.'

'And that's why you're not asleep?' exclaimed Mario, deeply upset. 'Oh, please. Go to sleep, go to sleep straight away. Now I know why I couldn't sleep myself. To calm myself down I have to hear you sleeping. Go on, put your mind at rest. We'll talk about all that tomorrow…' And he went to put out the light.

Giulio could hardly believe the kindness that was being poured down onto his bed. And he wanted to go on enjoying it. He stopped Mario putting the light out: 'You're more calm now. Why can't I have the reading now? Your throat is better? I haven't been sleeping well since there've been no more readings in the evening.'

And Mario, in complete good faith, since he no longer remembered his state of mind when success was certain and close and smiling upon him, exclaimed, 'I didn't know that. If I had I would have read to you every evening as much as and more than necessary. My bad throat wasn't much, and it's passed. If you want, I'll read De Amicis and Fogazzaro. And so you'll fall asleep quickly.'

This last remark gave the impression that by then the hoax

had already lost all its efficacy. If Gaia had been there he would have been discouraged and would have thought that any hoax would be vain against such presumption as that. On the contrary, in fact, at that moment, literature did not exist at all for Mario. All that existed was his sick brother, to whom he had to administer as much literature as was needed. And he was resigned to lowering the status of his own and other people's writings to the level of a clyster.

But that evening he did not wish to read. It was late, and he needed a few hours of sleep. He needed to be serene and rested when he met Gaia. And so instead of literature he made a present to Giulio of a different kind of affection. He treated him as a mother would, with authority and with the utmost tenderness, with commands and with promises. He told him that he had to sleep then, but that the next evening they would go back to their pleasant old custom. He would read him not only other people's works, but also works of his own of which he had never spoken and that he was now confiding to him. So many fables harvested in the most utter solitude. No one else could possibly suspect their existence. It was a homely sort of literature, born in the courtyard and destined for that room. Or rather it was not literature, because literature is something that is sold and bought. This was something for just the two of them and no one else. 'You'll see, you'll see. They're short, and so they're not suitable as lullabies. But I shall tell you, as I read them, how they were born, because every one of them records one of my days, or rather the rectification of the day. I have to repent of everything I did, but you will see that my thoughts were more shrewd than my actions.'

Soon afterwards Giulio was snoring, and Mario, pleased by his success with his brother, also fell asleep not much later. And to the violent hissing of the bora the rhythmical sounds coming from Giulio formed a refrain, as did, soon, some loud shouts from Mario, who, in his dreams, continued to be convinced that he deserved something else, that he deserved better. The hoax had not succeeded in altering his dream.

8

But early the next morning he got up and rediscovered his grief and his anger. The world, with the bora still raging under a dark sky, looked very sad to him, because it was bereaved of Westermann's existence.

His brother was still sleeping. He went up to his door. Mario smiled contentedly when he perceived that the sleeper's breathing had become less noisy during his long rest. He thought aloud, 'I'll be right back with you in less than no time, with you who love me.'

Struggling against the bora he set off in the direction of Gaia's house, situated in one of the roads parallel to the canal, quite deserted at that hour. He was about to go up to Gaia's, but then he changed his mind and went back onto the road. Those explanations must not have any witnesses. It was better to act as if the hoax – if there really had been a hoax – had not been broadcast. For a moment he would wait for Gaia on the road and then, if it were necessary, he would persuade him to follow him somewhere where he could be punished. What sort of places were they where it was possible to inflict punishment without creating a bad impression? Mario did not know. But, impractical as he was, he thought he had it all arranged. The important thing was to find Gaia.

He was lucky, anyhow. When he was already beginning to suffer from the intense cold, he saw the salesman appear. He was running. Having got home late as usual, he had stayed in bed until the last possible moment to arrive in time for work.

Mario, whose teeth were now chattering (even he did not know whether with the cold or the excitement), tackled him, having in mind relatively mild words with which to ask for an explanation. But Gaia had the misfortune not to be very attentive, perhaps because of his haste. Without greeting him, Mario asked him, 'Have you had any news of Westermann?'

The words he had prepared so carefully vanished, and Mario could not find any others. His whole organism was like a bow which, during the long impatient hours, had been drawn more and more to the limits of its resistance. He fired: he gave Gaia an enormous backhander across the face, such as he would not have believed his hand and arm capable of, since for long years they had not known any violent movement. The blow was so strong that it hurt his fist and arm too, and he almost lost his balance.

Gaia had lost his hat to the bora, which lifted it higher and higher. Now a hat, especially when the cold bora is blowing, is a very important object, and Gaia lost whatever little time to react he could have had, as he followed his hat with his eyes, uncertain whether he should run after it. That gave him, for an instant, an appearance of indifference which caused Mario to start in surprise. Perhaps he was mistaken? Perhaps Westermann did after all exist? And then what would he himself look like? There was an instant of anxiety and intense hope. His eyes still looked menacing, and yet he was thinking that a moment later he might have to throw himself at Gaia's feet.

But meanwhile Gaia's hat, after falling to the ground, rolled along the pavement and disappeared round the nearest corner.

It was on its way to the canal, to certain perdition, and Gaia knew that he could not recover it. He came up to Mario, having been driven away by the backhander, and Mario turned white as he realised that Gaia wanted to speak and not react violently. With all intelligent creatures it is to be observed that a strong physical pain, like that which the blow inflicted on Gaia, produces a strong sense of one's own wrongdoing. At the same time as Gaia protested, he confessed: 'Why? For playing an innocent prank?'

And so Mario learnt to his despair, but also to his relief, that Westermann definitely did not exist. He immediately confirmed the first backhander with another. And that would have been enough for him if his gentle mind had managed to intervene. But it is difficult, for anyone who lacks practice, to stop thumping when he has given himself up to it utterly and violently. And so on the head of the poor travelling salesman two further strong blows rained down, landed by Mario with both hands, because by now his left hand had to help his right hand, which was almost paralysed with pain.

At that point Gaia realised that he would have to resist, since if he did not it was difficult to tell when Mario would stop. He came up to Mario in a threatening way, but he was so weak that another blow struck him full in the face, even though he had parried it in time. He was also terrified by a hoarse shout from Mario, which seemed to him to signify an inhuman wrath. The shout had really been torn from Mario by the pain in his dislocated arm. Gaia's nose was bleeding and, under the pretext of covering it with his handkerchief, the wretched hoaxer had stopped look a p900 from Mario.

That was not a position well adapted for attack, but Mario did not notice. A poor working-class woman, quite rotund and all bundled up in her clothes, with a basket on her arm,

71

stopped to look at them. Gaia was ashamed, too, because Mario had at last found his tongue and was hurling insults at him: 'Drunkard, brazen-faced liar.' Gaia tried to put on a manly expression, but he could not, because he felt ill, very ill, and he was worried too. He knew for sure that he had been hit on the head, and he could not understand why his side hurt. If his head had been hurting he would not have been bothered. Panting, he said to Mario, 'Let's not act like louts. I am completely at your disposal.'

'You talk about honour, you?' shouted Mario. 'Aren't you even ashamed of the slaps you've had?' And at this point Mario at last found a way of saying the words with which he would have liked the explanations to begin: 'Bear in mind that if you divulge the hoax which you've dared to carry out, I'll let everyone know what's happened here and renew the treatment which you've just undergone, and add some kicks to it.' That reminded him that kicks, too, exist in this world, and he immediately inflicted one upon poor Gaia.

Gaia, repeating again and again that he was at Mario's disposal, and keeping half his face covered with his handkerchief, withdrew in the direction of his home, with menace in his eyes but inertia in his body. Mario did not pursue him, but turned his back on him in disgust.

He felt better, much better. Spiritual victories are no doubt very important, but a muscular victory is beneficial also. The heart acquires new confidence in the vessel in which it beats, it is put to rights and reinvigorated.

He went to his own office. The bora was blowing so strongly that on the canal bridge he had to stop and gather his forces before crossing it. And so he saw a spectacle which really cheered him up. Gaia's hat was sailing on the water, and, quickly enough, towards the open sea. It really was sailing. The sail was formed by part of the brim, which protruded above the water and caught the wind.

Then, like a man, he faced the unpleasant moment when he had to tell Brauer about the hoax. It was extremely easy. Brauer listened to him without batting an eyelid. He did not feel any surprise, because he still remembered how surprised he had been to learn that such a large sum had been offered for a novel. He applauded the first backhander given to Gaia, and at the second one he embraced Mario.

Then the unexpected happened. A discovery. It may happen to even the most practical men that they follow developments closely, having known all the facts from the start, and then find themselves amazed by a result which could have been foreseen, if they had put a few figures down on paper. Certain facts are lost for them in the blackness of night, when others nearby glitter with a too resplendent beam. Till now all the light had been poured out upon the novel, which was now sinking into the abyss, and a moment ago Brauer had remembered selling on behalf of Mario two hundred thousand crowns at an exchange rate of seventy-five. But the Austrian rate, in recent days, had weakened so much that, by that transaction, Mario found he had gained seventy thousand *lire*, precisely half of what he would have received if the contract with Westermann had been a valid one.

At first Mario shouted, 'I don't want that filthy money.' But Brauer was astonished and indignant. In commerce a literary man might have the right to draft a letter, but not to judge a matter of business. By refusing that money, Mario would show himself to be unworthy of any contribution to commerce.

When that huge sum was cashed, even Mario was full of admiration. Human life is strange, and mysterious; with this deal clinched by Mario almost unawares, the surprises of the post-war period began. Values shifted without rhyme or reason, and very many other innocents like Mario received the reward of their innocence, or, because they were so innocent, were destroyed. These were things which had always been known, but they seemed new because they were happening so often that they seemed almost to be the norm. And Mario, because of that money which he felt in his pocket, stood wondering in surprise, and analysed the situation. He was dazzled, and he murmured, 'It's easier to understand a sparrow's life than ours.' Who knows? Maybe our life looks so simple to the sparrows that they believe they can reduce it to fables?

Brauer said, 'That brute Gaia, if he had to devise such a hoax, should have based it on a sum of at least five hundred thousand crowns. Then you would have pocketed enough crowns to last your lifetime.'

Mario protested, 'And then I wouldn't have fallen for it. I would never have believed that anyone would pay so much for my novel.' Brauer was silent.

'I hope that my stroke of luck will not make the hoax I suffered better known,' said Mario anxiously.

Brauer reassured him. No one would have heard of his stroke of luck, because at the bank no one knew of the origin of the affair. In fact not even Gaia had got to know of it, because, if he had, he would very reasonably have asked for his five per cent commission.

The money came in useful for the two brothers. Given their modest way of life, it guaranteed them for many years, if not for ever, an easier life. And the face which Mario made when he cashed it was not repeated when he spent it. At times it even seemed to him that the money really did derive – as a highly esteemed prize – from his literary work. Nevertheless, his intellect, which was accustomed to take shape in exact words, did not let itself be deceived enough to bring him happiness.

This is shown by the following fable, with which Mario tried to ennoble his own money:

The swallow said to the sparrow, 'You are a contemptible creature, because you feed on the scraps you find lying about.' The sparrow replied, 'The scraps which feed my flight rise with me.'

Then, the better to defend the sparrow (with which he was identifying himself), Mario suggested to it another reply:

'It is a privilege to be able to feed even on things found lying about. You, who do not have this privilege, are forced into eternal flight.'

It looked as though the fable would never be finished, because long after, in a different kind of ink, Mario made the sparrow speak once more:

'You eat while you are flying, because you cannot walk.'

Mario modestly placed himself among the creatures that walk. These are very useful creatures that can, in truth, despise those that fly, whose pleasure in flying takes away any desire for improvement.

And the fable was not finished. On the contrary, it seems that he thought of that fable every time he felt how convenient it was to have so much money at his disposal. One day he became really furious with the swallow, which had only opened its beak one single time:

'Do you dare to reproach a creature because it is not made like you?'

So said the sparrow with its tiny brain. But if all creatures had been obliged to mind their own business and not impose their own propensities and even their organs on others, there would be no more fables in the world; and, beyond any doubt, this was not what Mario wanted.

Italo Svevo at
the British Admiralty

A Recollection by Umberto Saba

Translated by Estelle Gilson

Visiting my old antiquarian bookstore in Trieste today, I was once again struck by how much time and how many words it takes to close, or not close, even the smallest deal. When I arrived, the store's purchase of the *Children's Encyclopedia* was under discussion and the negotiations dragged on for at least another half hour to no avail. I remembered that in happier days (that is when it was I who was buying and selling), a 'yes' or 'no' was given more quickly.

I remembered, too, that about twenty years ago in the same place and on a similar occasion (endless negotiations between my stubborn assistant, Carletto, and an even more stubborn client), Italo Svevo told me, perhaps because of his love of contrasts, how things had gone with him in London when he closed the biggest deal of his life. A deal, I think, involving millions.

Italo Svevo (known in business as Ettore Schmitz) was a member of a Triestine firm that secretly manufactured and held exclusive rights for the sale of a mysterious product designed to protect the submerged parts of ships from the corrosive action of salt. The novelist, who by luck became famous just about the time he turned sixty, considered himself (and perhaps he was) a great businessman. I don't know if it was for that reason or because he knew English so well, but his firm gave him the responsibility of concluding negotiations already begun with the British Admiralty for its adoption of the celebrated underwater paint. This took place before the First World War when Trieste was Austrian and the English fleet was still enjoying its 'Nelsonian' reputation. To the world, it was 'the greatest naval force during peace'. For Trieste, every time the Mediterranean fleet anchored there peacefully, it meant festivities and guaranteed profits with, on the last night, fireworks on the wharves and from the great ships off the shore of that port of friendly trade. It was, to one and all, magical. Poor Schmitz, like everyone else, had fallen under the influence of that magic and climbed the steps of the austere Admiralty building with his heart pounding.

He was expected and was immediately taken into a small, cheerless and bare room that was more the size of a closet than an office. How impoverished England seemed to him from the inside. After a few minutes a young man in street clothes appeared and offered him the only available chair. The official himself sat on the table, which, together with the chair, made up the room's total furnishings. He crossed his long legs, offered perfumed cigarettes and lit them for himself and his guest, showed himself to be informed on the matter, asked two or three questions, then announced that everything seemed all right and that the deal was essentially concluded. Italo Svevo thought he was dreaming. He had anticipated a long string of documents, one more boring than the other, and a series of interminable discussions. And here it took only five minutes for his cherished underwater paint to be adopted by the most powerful navy in the whole world. In Italy or even France, he said, it would have taken five years. When he left the Admiralty (although the deal was completely honest and, as all really good deals are, advantageous to both parties), he fell prey to a vague sense of guilt. Yet, at the same time, it seemed to him that his feet had grown wings.

He was a dear man, old Schmitz. After the praise of his novels, especially printed praise, nothing pleased him as much as telling his friends stories of his long years in business. I heard more than one in the shop on the Via San Nicolò, where he used to drop in on me almost every evening, where the literati and (then) socially influential didn't disdain my conversation (if anything, the opposite applied), and which

I visit as seldom as possible today. May God and good Carletto forgive me, but now all it is to me is a dark hole crowded with ghosts. The author of *As a Man Grows Older* and *The Confessions of Zeno* seemed to be, and was, full of humanity, of (relative) understanding of others, and after his unexpected literary success, of an affecting *joie de vivre*.

In reality, he had an enormous fear of dying. Whether it was a joke or some kind of premonition, he never got into a taxi without giving the driver a strange piece of advice. 'Go slowly,' he'd say in Triestine dialect, 'you don't know who you've got in here.' (Naturally, he was referring to himself, no matter who was along with him.) He died, precisely (and strangely), as a result of an automobile accident. He wasn't hurt badly but his heart, which was weak (he attributed the weakness to his abuse of tobacco), couldn't withstand the trauma.

But Italo Svevo was always a lucky man. No sooner did he understand that he was dying and that he had really smoked that 'last cigarette', than his fear suddenly disappeared. 'Is this all there is to dying?' he asked his family. 'It's easy, very easy. It's easier,' he said, trying to smile, 'than writing a novel.'

I've always thought (and these words uttered by that man at that moment confirm my belief) that humour is the highest form of kindness.

Italo Svevo was born Ettore Schmitz into an Italian-German family in Trieste in 1861. He was educated in Trieste and at the Brüssel Institute near Würzburg in Germany, where he began to read German and Russian literature in earnest. On Schmitz's return to Trieste, his father, a rich glassware tradesman, tried to persuade him to join the family business, but Schmitz was already hoping to become a writer.

In 1880, Schmitz was forced to take work as a bank clerk when his father's business collapsed. He was to spend eighteen years at the bank, a period which provided the inspiration for his first novel, *Una vita* [*A Life*] (1893). At the age of thirty-seven, Schmitz married his cousin Livia Veneziani. It was a marriage which led him to change both religion – he converted from Judaism to Catholicism – and his career, joining the Venezianis' prosperous marine paint manufacturing business. The latter proved extremely successful for Schmitz, and he travelled widely as a salesman, setting up a branch of the company in England, and eventually took over the management of the paint business after the death of his father-in-law.

Schmitz published *Una vita*, his story of the futile life of a bank clerk, under the pseudonym Italo Svevo and at his own expense. It was a failure, and entirely ignored by critics. This did not deter him from producing a second novel, *Senilità* [*As a Man Grows Older*] in 1898, once more at his own expense, but, again, his work attracted no notice. Svevo was confused by the lack of critical attention and gave up on novels in order to devote himself to other works – fables, plays and short stories.

Svevo's literary silence was finally broken in 1907, when he met the young James Joyce, who was working as an English teacher in Trieste. Joyce took a great interest in Svevo's work, and they formed a lasting literary friendship. In 1912, Svevo discovered the work of Freud, which was to have an enormous influence on his subsequent literary output, and his final novel, *La coscienza di Zeno* [*The Confessions of Zeno*], an 'autobiography' of a man undergoing psychoanalysis for addiction, appeared in 1923. Once more, Svevo's work was ignored by critics and readers alike, but this time Joyce persuaded his French publishers to produce a translation of the novel, which received great praise. Finally Svevo was acknowledged in Italy, and drew the attention of the Italian writer and poet Eugenio Montale, who persuaded him to republish his earlier novels.

Svevo's work remained a subject of critical controversy, though it was now highly successful, and Svevo himself spent the last years of his life lecturing on his own writing. He had begun writing a sequel to *La coscienza di Zeno* when, in 1928, he died as a result of a car accident.

J.G. Nichols is a poet and translator. His published translations include the poems of Guido Gozzano (for which he was awarded the John Florio Prize), Giacomo Leopardi, and Petrarch (for which he won the Monselice Prize). He has also translated prose works by Ugo Foscolo, Giovanni Boccaccio, Giacomo Leopardi, Leonardo da Vinci, Luigi Pirandello, Giacomo Casanova, Giovanni Verga, Dante Alighieri and Gabriele D'Annunzio, all published by Hesperus Press.

HESPERUS PRESS – 100 PAGES

Hesperus Press, as suggested by the Latin motto, is committed to bringing near what is far – far both in space and time. Works written by the greatest authors, and unjustly neglected or simply little known in the English-speaking world, are made accessible through new translations and a completely fresh editorial approach. Through these short classic works, each around 100 pages in length, the reader will be introduced to the greatest writers from all times and all cultures.

For more information on Hesperus Press, please visit our website: **www.hesperuspress.com**

ET REMOTISSIMA PROPE

SELECTED TITLES FROM HESPERUS PRESS

Author	Title	Foreword writer
Pietro Aretino	*The School of Whoredom*	Paul Bailey
Jane Austen	*Love and Friendship*	Fay Weldon
Honoré de Balzac	*Colonel Chabert*	A.N. Wilson
Charles Baudelaire	*On Wine and Hashish*	Margaret Drabble
Giovanni Boccaccio	*Life of Dante*	A.N. Wilson
Charlotte Brontë	*The Green Dwarf*	Libby Purves
Mikhail Bulgakov	*The Fatal Eggs*	Doris Lessing
Giacomo Casanova	*The Duel*	Tim Parks
Miguel de Cervantes	*The Dialogue of the Dogs*	
Anton Chekhov	*The Story of a Nobody*	Louis de Bernières
Wilkie Collins	*Who Killed Zebedee?*	Martin Jarvis
Arthur Conan Doyle	*The Tragedy of the Korosko*	Tony Robinson
William Congreve	*Incognita*	Peter Ackroyd
Joseph Conrad	*Heart of Darkness*	A.N. Wilson
Gabriele D'Annunzio	*The Book of the Virgins*	Tim Parks
Dante Alighieri	*New Life*	Louis de Bernières
Daniel Defoe	*The King of Pirates*	Peter Ackroyd
Marquis de Sade	*Incest*	Janet Street-Porter
Charles Dickens	*The Haunted House*	Peter Ackroyd
Fyodor Dostoevsky	*Poor People*	Charlotte Hobson
Joseph von Eichendorff	*Life of a Good-for-nothing*	
George Eliot	*Amos Barton*	Matthew Sweet
F. Scott Fitzgerald	*The Rich Boy*	John Updike
Gustave Flaubert	*Memoirs of a Madman*	Germaine Greer
E.M. Forster	*Arctic Summer*	Anita Desai
Ugo Foscolo	*Last Letters of Jacopo Ortis*	Valerio Massimo Manfredi
Elizabeth Gaskell	*Lois the Witch*	Jenny Uglow

Robert Louis Stevenson	*Dr Jekyll and Mr Hyde*	Helen Dunmore
Theodor Storm	*The Lake of the Bees*	Alan Sillitoe
W.M. Thackeray	*Rebecca and Rowena*	Matthew Sweet
Leo Tolstoy	*Hadji Murat*	Colm Tóibín
Ivan Turgenev	*Faust*	Simon Callow
Mark Twain	*The Diary of Adam and Eve*	John Updike
Giovanni Verga	*Life in the Country*	Paul Bailey
Jules Verne	*A Fantasy of Dr Ox*	Gilbert Adair
Edith Wharton	*The Touchstone*	Salley Vickers
Oscar Wilde	*The Portrait of Mr W.H.*	Peter Ackroyd
Virginia Woolf	*Carlyle's House*	Doris Lessing
Virginia Woolf	*Monday or Tuesday*	Scarlett Thomas
Emile Zola	*For a Night of Love*	A.N. Wilson